PRAGUE, A SECRET FROM THE PAST

A CZECH TRAVEL MYSTERY

ADRIANA LICIO

The Home Travellers
Press

PRAGUE, A SECRET FROM THE PAST
A Czech Travel Mystery

Book 4 in the *The Homeswappers Mysteries* series
By Adriana Licio

Edition I
Copyright 2021 © Adriana Licio

Cover by **Wicked Smart Design**
Editing by **Alison Jack**

To Antonio Piccolo, our friend and vet,

I believe veterinarians work the double of any other doctor as for each furry patient they get at least one biped to take care of.

To his wife, Marica, and his children, Francesco, Vittoria and Edoardo, who generously give up a little of their father's time so he can help more animals.

CONTENTS

1

A NIGHT AT THE THEATRE

In one of the finest buildings close to Malostranské náměstí, the main square in Malá Strana, also known as the Lesser Quarter of Prague, a poor, dejected Basset Hound was curled up beneath a mahogany grand piano. He was all alone, betrayed by the human beings he had counted as his best friends thus far: two nasty women who'd had no scruples whatsoever in dragging him from his adoptive village of Castelmezzano in Southern Italy and abandoning him in this unknown city.

Mind you, it wasn't that the grandly named Napoleon, affectionately known as Leon, didn't enjoy discovering new places, or that he was missing home. Actually, he was very eager to get to know a little more of the wide world. But there was no way any self-respecting Basset Hound would discover much if, so soon after his arrival, his bipeds took him for a ridiculously short walk, then locked him in a strange house and disappeared. It was as if he counted for nothing within the family. Just another piece of luggage like one of the many bags the two mean humans had left scattered in the kitchen and their bedrooms.

Leon sighed so deeply that the piano strings vibrated in sympathy, amplifying his sense of forsakenness. To his credit, the hound was not only hurt by the abandonment, he was also seriously concerned about what might happen to the two women. They weren't used to being out and about without him to take care of them; they had no sense of orientation whatsoever, and more worryingly, they had a habit of getting into trouble. Oh no, trust this hound's hunch. This whole situation wasn't going to end well.

Leon squirmed to his feet, his body unwinding its entire length as he moved to the window. Getting up on his rear legs, he rested his paws on the window ledge, having a look out onto the street. The pavement was crowded with happy folk, strolling in the evening air, but he could not spot the two familiar figures of his bipeds.

He started to raise his eyes towards the sky, as if to remind Him to take care of his humans as Leon could not do that part of his job, but midway, his gaze was brought to an abrupt halt. A pair of soulful brown eyes was peering back at him from the building opposite: a pink palace on the other side of the road. Goodness, were they the eyes of a Basset? Certainly not as handsome as he was, but not bad.

Actually... the soft brown colour of the long ears, the concerned expression of the eyes, the pretty mouth... could it be...?

It could! He was looking at a very cute she-Basset.

As he pondered how his luck might be about to change, the she-Basset left the window, and he could hear her barking in happiness. Her humans must have arrived back home. Leon sighed. Only he... he was all alone again, with just his sadness and worry for company.

~

Mrs Concetta Natale Passolina, generally known as Etta, was sitting comfortably in a padded velvet chair in the majestic

National Theatre of Prague. Before taking her seat, she had noticed the daylight was still streaming in through the tall windows of the foyer. Up North in Europe, the days were getting longer, much longer than they were back home in Castelmezzano.

The theatre was an impressive building. Etta had almost felt overwhelmed when entering, courtesy of an invitation from the American Embassy, no less. A charming young woman by the name of Christine Coleman had arrived to greet them as Etta and her friend Dora were taking it all in: the large hall, the smartly dressed people, the crowds of Koreans with their severe expressions. Or at least, that's how they'd looked to Etta. Then Mrs Coleman, friend and Embassy colleague of the two women's homeswap partner, Patricia Parker, had introduced them to a huge number of people – Americans, Koreans, Czechs – and Etta had almost felt like a VIP when they all smiled at her.

The only drawback was now, they were all enjoying – or rather, enduring – a concert of traditional Korean music, and it wasn't to Etta's taste at all. The female musicians wore white shirts with shining gowns ballooning around their bodies, pink for those on the upper part of the stage, red for the women on the lower part. The male musicians were wearing pale green robes that reminded Etta of samurai costumes, their sleeves white and a darker green ribbon around their necks. It would have been quite fascinating, were it not for the fact that they were playing such unusual instruments. The singer was waving her fabric fan in the air as if it were her most precious possession while producing a series of strange sounds interspersed with sudden yowls that made Etta jump from her slumber. As much as she fought against it, she continually felt her head dropping, her eyelids closing, her whole body crying out for a long, deep, healthy sleep.

"GuGGGA, guGGGY, GGG, TZZT..." The singer went on, disturbing Etta violently. Then the flutes started shrieking like chalk on a blackboard. It wouldn't do to doze off, not now when her host Mrs Coleman could be around. Etta had to think of something to keep herself awake.

And her mind soon went to Leon, the Basset she and her friend Dora had left home alone an hour earlier. The funny dog had given them such a disapproving look, acting like a spoiled brat. Of course, before leaving him in what was to be their home for the duration of their stay in Prague, the two women had taken him for a long walk, leaving their unpacking until later for his sake. After a lengthy drive from Trento where Dora's cousin Angelina lived, the dog really deserved a bit of fresh air, even more so as he would be on his own for the rest of the evening.

It had been nice to discover part of the Malá Strana quarter, the Vltava River, the castle perched up above their new home. The dog's hunch had led them towards a park along the river, which they discovered to be part of the Kampa Island, festooned with an explosion of lilac flowers in a multitude of shades. Etta had never thought such natural beauty possible in the middle of a city.

What was meant to be just a short walk in the neighbourhood had turned into an exhausting hike to keep the hound happy. Excited to discover a new place, he had kept pulling them along eagerly, but once they had finally returned home and he realised the two women were about to leave him, he had sulked at them. But then, he would do that even when one of them left him to take the rubbish out, he was such a goon.

"GuGGGA, guGGGY, GGG, TZZT." The singer squawked, the piano clunked, the flute squealed, and Etta's red hair fell over her face as her head landed heavily on her chest.

~

MISS DOROTEA ROSA PEPE, OR SIMPLY DORA, WAS CLASPING HER hands, her salt-and-pepper fringe parted in the middle, her mouth open like that of a cod that had been left out of the water too long. Her heart was beating furiously in her chest. It was all too perfect: Prague, a city she had dreamed about for years, had unfolded in front of her dreamy eyes as Leon had scampered along, pulling her with him.

The invitation to the concert in the sumptuous National Theatre was the cherry on the cake, the musicians playing their traditional instruments and narrating the story of life in a rural Korean village. The unusual tunes were taking Dora on a journey across the Far East, the singer's shrill voice transcending time and place and inviting her soul to rise well above the mundanity of real life...

It was a year since Dora had left her ugly flat in the only ugly building in Pietrapertosa, a village perched high in the mountains in Southern Italy, and moved in to live with her friend Etta in her beautiful home in Castelmezzano. By sharing expenses, they'd been able to live a more dignified life than their paltry teachers' pensions would have allowed them to do alone. But even better, they had joined the Home Swapping Circle International and started to travel all around Europe, discovering exciting places and making new friends.

Ah, being in her sixties and realising that life could still be this generous to her, that there was (almost!) no limit to the things she could achieve, was wonderful. And Etta had become a good friend, creating a real bond of sisterhood. Then, in Rothenburg ob der Tauber, they had met Napoleon, the funny, generous, touchy Basset. He was sulking at them now, she knew that, as they had left him all alone, although they had treated him to a long, long walk around Prague beforehand. Still, Leon had his own peculiar way of marking the passage of time, minutes alone being 10 times longer than those spent with his friends...

Dora's reverie was interrupted by a strange low sound. What on earth was it? Whatever it was, it had caused quite a few spectators to turn their eyes towards them. It wasn't the orchestra, Dora was sure. It was more like an OINK!

Turning her head towards her companion, Dora found Etta fast asleep, her head sagging in to her chest. Powerful snores were rising into the air, resonating with a deep F3 and harmonising with a high E from the singer.

2

PEOPLE, CHAMPAGNE AND BUBBLES

W hen the curtains fell and the audience had finished applauding the musicians and singers, the crowd gently swayed towards the entrance hall. There, Christine Coleman approached Etta and Dora, asking whether they had enjoyed the show.

"Are you joking?" cried Etta. "My ears have not yet recovered..."

"It was most exciting." Dora spoke over her friend's blunt words. "I had never heard anything like that before."

"Yes, Gugak music is traditionally Korean, quite different from what we're used to in the West."

"Wildly different," said Etta.

"I could really picture myself in some Korean garden with a pagoda and ponds and a little wooden bridge crossing the slowly flowing water. Some red-leafed maples and..."

Etta looked at her friend in amazement. Was Dora just being a people pleaser as usual, or had she really pictured all that she was describing? And more to the point, why hadn't she, Etta, felt anything like that?

"...and the National Theatre is simply gorgeous," Dora concluded.

"I'm so glad you enjoyed it all, and I hope you will stay for dinner."

The two friends looked at each other. As nice as the offer sounded, they were both thinking of a certain disgruntled hound back home.

"I'm afraid we can't, we left our dog all alone almost as soon as we arrived. It's a new home for him, too…"

"Oh, you travelled all that way with a dog? How interesting. But please, it's just a few light refreshments served at the theatre bar. Come for a drink at least and I'll see if I can introduce you to someone interesting."

As she spoke, Christine guided them along the opulent foyer with its magnificent doors on both sides, marble floors, frescoed ceiling and luscious crystal lamps suspended over small tables. She looked around as they walked, evidently wondering who could be suitable company for the two women. There were plenty of businesspeople, but no doubt they'd be more interested in setting up commercial relationships between the Czech Republic and the United States or South Korea than chatting to a couple of sexagenarian holidaymakers.

The Korean Ambassador passed by and Christine introduced the gentleman. Like many Koreans, he was a lover of opera and found quite a lot to discuss on the subject with Dora, whilst Etta didn't feel she had much to say to any of the folks around her. She simply nodded and tried hard to smile.

A woman in a full-length red evening dress approached the group. Probably in her fifties, she had long blonde hair held tightly in a neat chignon and seemed to be the most beguiling presence in the whole room. Certainly she was a woman who had caught Etta's attention.

"Ambassador," Christine said, "may I have the pleasure of introducing you to Ms Eva Kladivova? Since the Velvet Revolution, she has transformed one of our nationalised companies into a private one and relished all changes and challenges that entails."

"It's my pleasure, Ambassador," the woman said, but there was something so charismatic about her, it was obvious the pleasure was actually all on the Ambassador's side.

"Ms Kladivova's company now has a number of customers in the United States. She's possibly one of the most successful exporters in the electrical equipment industry. I'm sure she would be interested in partnering with Korean firms as well..."

Before Christine could go into more details about Ms Kladivova's company, another man approached them.

"I beg your pardon, but here's Mike Smolak of the US Department of Commerce. He's helped us set up the conference and roadshow that will take place in the next few days."

A sturdy man in his late fifties, the newcomer was wearing a smart black dress suit and a bow tie. Despite the fact he spoke with a predominantly American accent, a certain hesitation and occasional unusual speech pattern revealed he was, in all likelihood, Czech. His deep blue eyes lingering on Etta and Dora, he shook hands with them, extolling the pleasure of meeting the dear Italian friends of his colleague at the Embassy, Patricia Parker. Etta felt some magnetic power emanating from him, along with a sense of humour evident in his sparkling expression.

After a couple of gentle questions about their home and country, Mike's attention was drawn elsewhere as more people joined their group. Etta and Dora started to feel like fish out of water as the conversation revolved around international trade agreements, industry challenges and cooperation between countries. Luckily, Christine noticed and, quick as flash, requested permission to introduce the two Italians to some more people.

"Look, there's dearest Marketa! She made it after all."

The woman Christine was pointing out was not only as short and round as Etta and Dora, she was obviously about the same age. This alone created some common ground, and Etta's interest was piqued still further when Christine introduced Marketa as the Embassy Nurse during the Velvet Revolution years, now enjoying her retirement.

Marketa was speaking animatedly to a lanky man who wore a shabby suit and no tie.

"This is Mr Egon Zima," Christine said as she approached with her two guests. "Long time, no see, Egon."

"Oh yes, you're right, I don't attend the Embassy that much nowadays," Mr Zima said, nodding to Christine.

"But you should! We're always ready to help Czech companies find good partners abroad..."

"That's why I'm here," the man said.

"I hope the ladies won't mind if I take you away for a few minutes. There are some interesting people I'd like you to meet," said Christine, taking Egon's arm and pointing to the group Etta and Dora had just left.

"Oh no, please do," said Dora. "We're aware it's a business meeting, after all; we don't want to get in the way."

"I will take care of them," said Marketa. Christine flashed her a smile, and then led Mr Zima towards the group.

"So, you're from Italy?" Marketa said.

"Not our fault," said Etta, winking at her.

"Oh, Italy!" Marketa cried, her hazel eyes sparkling in wonder. "I had to book one of those coach tours. I've been begging my friends for years to come with me to visit the country, but you know what? People of my age are ready to do anything when you suggest it, but as soon as the moment comes to do it for real – book a ticket, select a hotel – that's when they discover they cannot leave their granddaughters and grandsons; their houses need maintenance; their husbands cannot cope alone. So I gave up on them and joined a coach tour travelling to Venice, Florence and Rome..."

"And how about your own husband and grandchildren?" Dora asked.

"My goodness, I wouldn't have made such a big mistake. I

never got married. I liked a few men when I was young, but trust me, none of them was worth marrying."

"I wish I had been that clever," said Etta, thinking of her former husband. She'd endured quite a few years with him before realising she'd be better off with no man than a pathetic specimen, building a new life for herself and Maddalena, her only daughter. It had not been easy, but at least it had been the end of the lies, cheating and quarrels.

"I'm sure not all men are that bad." Dora had never married, instead taking care of her father, a man with boundless charm coupled with a gambling habit that had completely depleted the family wealth.

"Of course they are," said the other two resolutely, continuing to talk about the misdeeds of the male species.

The champagne that was being passed around was bubbly, refreshing and delicious. Surely it could not contain much alcohol? Before long, the three women's table was the one that rang with the most laughter and jokes. Others around the room were smiling at them indulgently, but their good humour certainly contributed to making the atmosphere less formal and more relaxed.

Etta was still indulging in her new favourite hobby of declaring men to be the most spineless creatures on earth when her eyes wandered again to Eva Kladivova, the woman in red. She was standing where Etta and her companions had left her, talking with the Korean Ambassador who had been joined by his wife. Mr Smolak and Egon Zima were also there, but what a transformation had come over the woman's face. Her eyes scrutinising the length of the room, she glared in the direction of a man in a black suit, a cheesy grin on his face. Her jaw tightening, her attractive face had screwed up and deformed into an expression of unequivocal hatred.

Etta was stunned. There was something so strong, so primitive in Ms Kladivova's gaze. It was impossible to dismiss it.

The woman, as if suddenly aware she was showing more

emotion than was proper, lowered her head and searched for something in her bag. She drew out a packet of cigarettes, putting one into her mouth without lighting it. She was obviously trying to regain her composure, but was failing miserably. To Etta at least, she had lost all the serene strength she had displayed earlier.

The man in the black suit marched all the way from one end of the long foyer to the other. He nodded to Eva Kladivova, who ignored him, and then approached Etta's group.

"Marketa dear," he said, addressing the nurse.

"Josef Janda, is that really you?" Marketa said in surprise. "Such a pleasure to see you again."

"It's been years, but I see you're just as humorous and strong-minded as ever." He looked at her with admiring eyes as the two of them lapsed into speaking Czech, a language neither Etta nor Dora was familiar with. Still, they could not help but notice the pair chatted with the comfortable ease of old friends.

After a while, obviously feeling she was leaving her new friends out of the conversation, Marketa said, "Mr Janda is from Brno where he owns a factory. We were good friends at the time of the Velvet Revolution. He used to come to the… US Embassy every now and then." She paused briefly before naming the Embassy. The man flushed a little, and Etta could not help asking one of her blunt questions.

"Are you in the same line of business as Ms Kladivova?"

"Indeed I am, but she's a ruthless competitor. She's hardly left us any room for negotiation with US companies…" He said that with a shy smile. "Actually, I'd better try to catch Mr Smolak before he promises all his support to her company only. But you, Marketa… I'll be in Prague for the whole week, taking part in the conference the Embassy has organised, and I'd love to see more of you."

"Certainly," Marketa replied, giving him her phone number.

By the time Josef Janda joined Ms Kladivova and Mr Smolak's group, the woman had almost entirely recovered. Her gaiety had been compromised, but she had managed to hide her earlier expression of spite. She actually greeted Mr Janda, albeit with a contemptuous smile that contrasted with his more amenable manner.

It was then that Etta's eyes moved from the group of people to the clock behind the bar.

"Eleven o'clock!" she cried in horror.

"Really?" shrieked Dora. "We'd better leave at once, poor Leon has been alone all this time."

They exchanged contact details with Marketa and left with promises to meet very soon for coffee so she could be their guide on a native's eye tour of Prague. Then they said goodbye to Christine, who told them they must come and visit the Embassy; it was normally closed to the general public, but open to visitors by invitation. All she asked was that they waited until the conference had finished.

∼

ONCE THEY WERE OUTSIDE, THE NIGHT AIR DID NOTHING TO CLEAR Etta and Dora's heads. They felt happily befuddled with champagne, debating for longer than was strictly necessary whether to call for a taxi or not. But they'd had a long journey across Europe to get to Prague, and every little they could save would help. After all, their new home was only a couple of kilometres away, and Christine had told them time and time again how safe Prague was, even at night, even for women. Certainly, they had to keep an eye out for the occasional pickpocket, but in general, the centre of Prague was much safer than other cities.

"Do you think we'll be able to find the way back home?" wondered Etta.

"It's almost straight ahead. Once we're on Charles Bridge, it'll be easy to find our way."

"Let's go, then."

And Prague welcomed them once more with all the charms of its night lights, the bridges on the Vltava, the castle on a hill in the distance. From the Charles Bridge, the two towers of the Lesser Town, one short and Romanesque, the other slender and Gothic, emerged from the darkness. The statues on the sides looked like mysterious creatures, while the reflection of a fat moon undulated over the silken waters of the river. This all merged into an irresistible combination of romance and mystery, of gloom and beauty.

"Ahh!" cried Dora, clasping her hands. She was enraptured. This was happiness; this was feeling at one with the whole universe. Her skin was covered with goosebumps, overtaken as she was by the emotion of so much beauty. She stood there, unable to move until Etta, for once gently, reminded her of the doggy waiting for them at home.

～

LEON HAD BEEN COUNTING EVERY SINGLE MINUTE, WONDERING HOW many days, maybe weeks, had passed since the two traitors had locked him in a strange flat. He squirmed and sighed.

Then suddenly, he sensed them coming. They weren't that close, but they were not too far away, either. He went to the window where his eyes confirmed what he had sensed as he saw two figures wobbling along the street. Their demeanour was a little odd, but there was no mistake: the bipeds were nearly home.

Then he heard them entering the main door from the street into the building and getting in the lift. Quickly, he reviewed his strategy. He would stay put under the piano, pretending he were at death's door, starved. Too weak to move, he would not even turn his head towards them. Actually, he would keep it down and his eyes closed, wouldn't deign to give them so much as a look. That would teach them a lesson once and for all.

He heard the key turn in the lock, and before he'd even

finished his list of resolutions, his body had jumped up from the floor, his mouth woofing and whining like a puppy. Standing in front of the door to welcome them, he wagged his stupid tail in such a frenzy, he could have whipped egg whites into the firmest of peaks. His long body was swaying from right to left and back. But then again, Bassets' tails are famous for having a life of their own, neither knowing nor caring what the rest of the body wants to do.

"Dear Leon," said Dora, giving him a loud smacking kiss on the head.

"He will wake up the entire building," said Etta, determined to hide how happy seeing the doggy's delight made her.

After a short pee-only walk, they all went to bed, but Leon lay awake for a while, thinking about his own conduct. Had he been a weak Basset and a bad educator? Then he recalled Lesson 7 of the *Canine Handbook to Training Perfect Humans*. The whole chapter was dedicated to the use of positive reinforcement techniques: ignore humans when they were misbehaving – when they left you all alone in the house, for example – and praise them when they did the right thing, like coming back. So, he had been a consistent instructor after all, but goodness! If educating humans wasn't a tough responsibility.

3

AN EARLY WALK

Etta jumped from her bed. Something cold and unyielding was pressing against her neck, scaring the life out of her. It was only seconds later that she realised it wasn't a deadly weapon at all; it was Leon's nose.

She settled back under the covers. "Please, let me sleep."

For an answer, Leon buried his cold, wet nose even more deeply into her neck, his front paws scrabbling inside the duvet. When that got no reaction, he grabbed the duvet and pulled it onto the floor, engaging the sleepy Etta in a tug of war.

"OK, you win!" she cried. Finally getting up, she moved to the kitchen, desperate for coffee, the champagne bubbles still blurring her vision and senses.

"Doraaaaa!"

"Yes, dear?" The woman always had a kind word, even first thing in the morning, while the best Etta could manage to share with the world was a grump and an uncharitable thought.

"The dog wants to go out."

"I'll be ready in five minutes." But Etta could hear from Dora's voice that she too would rather get some more sleep. The champagne had affected them both.

They met on the threshold, light coats thrown over their

pyjamas. In the lift, they kept yawning, whilst Leon... well, Leon was happy, rested, full of energy and determined to get to know Prague's every corner.

When they opened the large, heavy door, the sky was a soft pastel colour, the air chilly, and the whole of Malostranské náměstí seemed strangely quiet and empty. They now had the chance to notice its cobblestones and buildings, its arcades and the façade of San Nicholas church with all its statues. Even the shops in the always busy Mostecká Street were closed; in fact, there were very few people around, despite the fact the street led towards the popular Charles Bridge.

"What the heck?" cried Etta, looking at her watch. She shook it in impatience – the stupid thing must have stopped – and raised her eyes in search of a clock, finding a cast iron Art Nouveau timepiece on yet another empty cobbled street. "Quarter to six?"

Dora looked just as lost. "That'll be why there's hardly anyone in the street."

Etta looked fiercely straight into the Basset's innocent droopy eyes.

"You... betrayer! You're supposed to be a man's – or a woman's – best friend, not their tormentor."

For an answer, Leon trotted along, happy as ever.

They had just passed the two towers that gave access to the bridge, the sun dawning ahead of them, when Leon pulled to the right, aiming towards Kampa Park. This time, both women combined their efforts to stop him.

"No way! We're not missing this chance to walk on Charles Bridge when it's almost empty."

There were no musicians, no souvenir sellers; just a few walkers hurrying along – probably local people on their way to work, who would only dare to cross the bridge at that time of day when the visiting crowds were still tucked up in their beds – and a few tourists who had spent the whole night drinking and were now, in the fresh air of the morning, trying to find the strength to return to their hotels. Dora stood lost in wonder, her hands clasped, in front of the statue of St Francis with its two angels. Her mouth was open in a silent "Wow!"; only her eyes moved from the Old Town Tower and the spires in the distance, along the waters of the Vltava, back to the cobbled bridge, which would never look more beautiful than it did in this soft light, and on to the northern side: the Mánesův Bridge and the glittering golden Rudolfinum concert hall.

Etta took Leon's leash from her friend's hand. She knew from experience that as long as the trance lasted, Dora could quite easily lose her bag as well as the hound. In fact, she could even be undressed and have all her clothes and belongings taken without realising it.

As the rapture looked set to last a while, Etta moved closer to the statue of St Francis, enjoying the view without transforming into a levitating Buddha in the middle of the bridge. Leon, curious as ever to gaze down on his choice of destination, the park just below them, jumped up and placed his front legs on the bridge-side wall.

But the view was not what either Etta or Leon had expected.

~

A NUMBER OF PEOPLE WERE MOVING AROUND JUST BELOW THEM AND a couple of police cars and an ambulance were parked a few metres away.

"What's happening?" wondered Etta. And then she spotted a glimpse of a red robe on the ground between the legs of the people in uniform. "Let's move on, Saint Teresa," she cried at Dora, whose expression reminded her of that on the face of Bernini's sculpture, the *Ecstasy of Saint Teresa of Avila*. Taking her arm abruptly, Etta dragged her friend in the direction Leon had wanted to go all along.

Down the steps they went. Setting their feet once more on the Island of Kampa, they passed the pretty Shrine of Eternal Flame,

Etta pulling Dora along assertively before she took the chance to stop to look up at it again. They passed the proud statue of Bruncvik – the legendary Czech prince who travelled the world – and a few buildings until they came to a little jetty. There, standing amongst the trees scattered around, a man in uniform barred their way.

"I'm afraid, madam, you'll have to go back and make a detour on the other side."

"I'm afraid, *sir*," Etta mocked him, "I know the woman who appears to have drowned in the river."

"Really?"

"Do I look like someone who enjoys stupid jokes at 6am?" *Maybe that wasn't the right question to ask*, she mused, *when you're wearing your coat over your pyjamas, your face shows that it's the morning after a jolly night before, you're dragging along a woman in an equally bad condition and your Basset Hound looks like he's possessed by a demon.* Nonetheless, something in her imperious voice worked its magic.

"I'll tell the Lieutenant." The policeman addressed one of his colleagues in Czech, and seconds later, the other officer was eyeing them suspiciously.

"My colleague tells me you know the victim," he said dubiously, taking in the trio's appearance.

Etta breathed in deeply, pushed her large red glasses up her nose and adopted her best you-donkey-I-am-a-teacher tone.

"I fear so. Of course, I cannot be one hundred per cent sure, but I recognised that long red dress with its train. I don't think there were too many women out in that attire last night, but I might be wrong."

"And who may she be?"

Etta told him about the concert at the National Theatre. She must have sounded trustworthy enough, because he then asked her if she would mind coming along with him to identify the body.

The Police Lieutenant went ahead to speak to the forensic

team around the body, then a doctor stepped back so that Etta could see the woman lying on the riverbank. It was just as she'd feared: the face, as wet and frozen and colourless as it was, was unmistakably that of Ms Eva Kladivova.

"The poor woman fell into the river," cried Dora in shock.

"I don't think so," Etta replied. "Someone pushed her in."

The Lieutenant had done his best up until now to keep a cool demeanour, but he could not contain his surprise at Etta's words. He raised suspicious eyes to hers.

"How do you know that?"

"Two things. One, as you yourself said, we know the *victim*. I'm not sure you'd use that word for a suicide. Secondly, from the little I know of her, she was not the type of woman to do herself in. Actually, she was determined to network for her company, get ahead of the competition, weave new business relationships…"

"Do we have a new Jessica Fletcher?" The cop smirked below his thick moustache.

"Pah! I don't write books – what a tedious job, sitting at a table for hours, making up stories. No, I definitely prefer to go out and enjoy real life."

Oh, how Etta loved to speak for effect. The Czech detective wasn't to know she had spent the entire winter giving extra tuition to students, a couple of whom were so hopelessly dumb, she had felt like sitting them in front of the pigsties on Enzo's farm back in Castelmezzano in the hope some form of intelligence would make its way from the animals into their brains by osmosis. But then, that was how she and Dora had managed to save enough money for their big European adventure. Life needed its boring parts to contrast with the excitement of travelling – but the officer did not need to know any of that.

"A real adventuress, I see," he said. "I'm Lieutenant Jan Baloun, by the way, and I do need to take a statement from you. Just let me have a few more words with the forensics, and I'll get back to you." Then he turned towards a policewoman who had been hanging about behind him throughout the conversation. "Štičková, how good is your English?" he asked her.

"Quite good, sir," the woman said, flushing slightly.

"Then you take care of these two women and their dog. Ask the bar owner if we can use that table there, there're no people around yet. Start by taking their details and I'll join you soon." He then gave her a few more instructions, this time in Czech, concluding in English, "And order me a coffee, too."

The policewoman, her light brown hair in a ponytail under her hat, accompanied Etta, Dora and Leon to the bar. They sat outside; the sun was shining, but the day hadn't started to warm yet and they were glad of the coffee. When the Lieutenant joined them, he sat at an angle so that he could keep an eye on the forensics team finishing their job.

"Details taken?"

"Yes. I've scanned their docs, too, and taken their Prague address. They actually live quite close to the police station, should we need to speak to them again."

Baloun had a look at their details, then Dora and Etta had to explain the home swap thing. Neither police officer commented, but they did raise their eyebrows as if they were hearing about something out of the ordinary. Then Etta told them about the concert they had attended the previous evening, the hour they'd passed in the bar afterwards, who they had been introduced to.

Etta hesitated.

"Is there something more you want to add?" the Lieutenant asked her.

"Well, I'm not sure whether I should say this…"

"If you're in doubt, better say it."

"That's not so easy."

"Why?"

"Again, two reasons."

"Please explain," the policeman said with a wry smile.

"One, I might shed suspicions on someone based on a fleeting impression that could be wrong."

"As I said, you really must be Jessica Fle…"

"Two," Etta cut him short, "you police might think I'm nothing more than an imaginative old lady, playing sleuth."

"Well," the detective seemed to sink into deep thought. After a long, studied pause, he looked at his colleague, then back at Etta. "As for point one, we'll take into consideration that there's a slight possibility you might be wrong. As for two, I can reassure you, I never missed an episode of *Murder, She Wrote*."

"You devil!"

"Please do not interrupt a Prague Lieutenant's train of thought, he might never catch up with it again!" A flash of laughter made his eyes twinkle. "And I've always thought how dumb the police were, never to consider all Jessica Fletcher discovered and revealed. You can be assured, I'll not fall into that trap myself. Will I, Štičková?"

The young policewoman's nod was somewhat forced. To Etta, it was clear Štičková was not sure which lecture at the Police Academy had covered being this playful with a key witness. Or was the Lieutenant serious? It was difficult to tell what the man really had in mind.

"OK, then," Etta conceded, and she told them about the look of pure hatred she'd seen on the victim's face when Josef Janda had walked into the room. "Of course, it might mean nothing…"

"…or everything, we'll have to see."

Before letting them go, Baloun asked Etta to draw a simple plan of the theatre foyer on a napkin and specify where she had been standing, and where the people she had mentioned had been.

"This is precious – file it as a critical document," he said, handing the crumpled paper napkin to a dumbfounded Štičková.

"Yes, sir," she replied, on the verge of either laughter or

despair. It was obvious she'd rather be speaking to the pathologist and searching for clues.

"Did the pathologist confirm that Eva Kladivova died by drowning in the Vltava?" Etta asked. The Lieutenant's attitude had convinced her he would be amenable to her asking questions.

"Oh, there she is, already at work. You see, Štičková, we could go on holiday and leave these quiet ladies to do our job."

"Sir?"

"I'm sure they'll get there before we do." Returning his stare to Etta, he said, "So, how did the murderer kill her? You're right, the first thing the pathologist said was that he'd have to see if the woman was already dead when she hit the water. We'll only know that for sure after the post-mortem. But… the fellow has found a stab wound in her back. The killer wanted to make sure he did his job properly: he stabbed her, and then threw her into the river. Maybe he didn't expect the currents to return the body to the bank so soon, and possibly close to the spot where the murder took place."

"What about the time of death?"

"Hard to say because of the water temperature, but the doctor says between midnight and 4am. Possibly after the post-mortem, the pathologist will return a more accurate time of death." He rose from the table. "Ladies, I have your contact details should I need more insights from you and your dog. Are you sure I can't offer him a chocolate croissant?"

"Never!" cried Etta in horror.

"Mate, I did my best." The Lieutenant offered his condolences to the poor Basset Hound, whose ears had gone into free fall at Etta's response.

∼

MOVING ON ALONG THE RIVER BANK, ETTA, DORA AND LEON PASSED the Liechtenstein Palace and entered what had already become the hound's favourite place: the Kampa park with its century-old trees and lilacs in all shades from white to purple, from pale pink to light blue.

"Could you ever imagine we'd find a policeman with a sense of humour?" Etta asked.

"I wasn't sure when he was being serious and when he wasn't."

"I believe he takes a degree of pleasure in confusing his young trainee."

Dora couldn't help a smile; she'd noticed that too. Then she remembered that they had also encountered a murder victim, and the smile faded away.

"Poor Eva, to be killed in such a brutal way."

"Well, you can't be killed in a nice way, can you?"

"No, that's true, but that woman... she seemed so full of life..."

"You should have seen the way she looked at Mr Janda, though. I wonder what happened between the two of them in the past."

"Christine seemed to know her quite well."

"Yes, we might have to have a little chat with her... but what's up with the dog?" Etta asked, seeing the hound pulling at the leash, his nose on the ground, his tail well up and whipping the air in excitement.

"I really don't know," Dora replied, inviting Leon to slow down a bit. They had reached the southern end of the Kampa park, and as far as the two bipeds were concerned, they were ready to walk back home.

"There must have been a dog he liked. A female dog, I guess."

Female dog or not, Leon was of another mind. Bassets have a stubborn quality that is second to none, and their power to pull is definitely not proportionate to their outward appearance. Deaf to all pleas to slow down and behave civilly, he dragged forward relentlessly. He gave Dora no chance to stop to breathe in the scent of the lilacs, nor admire the views of the old town facing the Vltava River, not enthuse over the unique shape of Charles Bridge and its towers, nor clasp her hands in rapture at the carpet of spires and red roofs. Nope, the Basset had only one thing in mind, and he kept following his instincts.

Before the two women knew what was going on, they were up on Most Legii, the Legion bridge further up that crossed the Střelecký ostrov (the Archers' island). Leon finally stopped just before the island. On the bridge was a sort of balcony projecting out onto the Vltava where people could admire rows of horse chestnut trees along the river and the Kampa island, the white façade of the Kampa museum and all the parks around it. It looked more like a rural scene than the middle of a city.

Only one of the three wasn't bothered at all with sightseeing and pretty views. His nose still glued to the ground, Leon was sniffing and scratching with his paw. Finally, he managed to get the attention of his bipeds.

"Look, Etta, what's this?" said Dora, kneeling down with caution, fearing at her age that getting up again might not be so easy. She pointed at a small object that looked like a lipstick compact. "Do you think it might be possible that…"

"Wait, don't touch it," said Etta, taking a couple of pictures before picking it up using one of Leon's poo bags. The compact was speckled gold on the outside, the inside lined with red silk and containing a little mirror and a deep flamenco-red lipstick. "I'd think it was a weird coincidence that Leon should find this, but if we walk past this island, won't we be just in front of the theatre?"

Leon agreed. He had some more sleuthing to do, pulling his bipeds along the bridge until they recognised the loaf-shaped roof of the theatre, dark blue with shining stars and a rectangular golden crown rising above the island trees.

As they left the Archers' Island behind, they admired the ochre theatre building in its entirety, with its porches, arched windows, statues decorating the terrace, and the chariot and horses on its tower. That is, they would have admired the majestic theatre if it hadn't been for Leon launching himself into the traffic and crossing the road towards the Café Slavia. Fortunately, Prague drivers, who seem to excel at driving at full speed whenever they have a few metres of road ahead of them, have a sacred respect for pedestrian crossings. Even when, as in Leon's case, the pedestrian just strolls into the road without looking right or left.

Leon didn't even notice the screech of brakes of a passing tram. Growing up in the ancient streets of Rothenburg ob der Tauber, he had never learned to fear cars, but Etta's heart jumped into her throat as she imagined the three of them being squashed as flat as gingerbread figures. But the tram driver, instead of hurling insults from the window of his cab, however justified they may have been, greeted them with a friendly smile.

And then, by some form of miracle, they not only landed safely on the pavement in front of the Café Slavia, they also found themselves nose to nose with Mr Josef Janda.

4

MR JOSEF JANDA

"Miss Dora, Mrs Etta." The man greeted them in this quaint manner, finding their surnames too difficult to remember.

"Good morning, Mr Janda."

"I was worried that tram was going to run you over."

"I'd say we've already had enough drama for one day," Etta replied bluntly.

"Are you on your way to work?" Dora interjected. If the man didn't know what had happened to Eva Kladivova, there had to be a gentler way of telling him.

He smiled. "No, I'm an early riser, although I am attending the US business conference later on today. I love to see Prague when it's still sleepy, it's such a charming city. Don't you think?"

"It is," said Etta as grudgingly as she could. She was instantly distrustful of this man, all cuteness and big smiles.

"Oh," said Dora, looking around once more, "I believe it's the most romantic of the European capitals."

Etta was going to remind her friend she had not visited enough European capitals to say that with any conviction, but on seeing that Josef Janda seemed delighted by her friend's heartfelt admiration, she wondered if it might not be the perfect strategy to catch him unaware.

"I could stand for hours on one of those bridges and take it all in," Dora continued.

"That's so very true," the man agreed.

"Well, I rather hope we won't stand *here* for hours," said Etta pointedly. The number of pedestrians strolling past the café was increasing by the minute, making the pavement rather crowded.

"How about a little breakfast at the Slavia?" Janda suggested. "That is in itself an experience no visitor should miss."

Etta and Dora looked at each other. They had to be careful with managing their money – they had a long journey waiting for them when they left Prague. But cafés were much less expensive than restaurants, and if they took great care to have most of their meals at home, especially the more expensive dinners, they could treat themselves to a coffee and a pastry. As if in agreement, their stomachs started to grumble in anticipation.

"Will they allow Leon in?" Dora asked, as Etta's mind calculated the prices displayed in Czech koruna on the menus in the café's window.

"Certainly, we Czechs love our pets. Come on in for a real Prague breakfast."

The café was a triumph of Art Deco, all marble, mirrors and wood. Some black and white photos hung on the walls, a reminder of the city's splendours, and of the important visitors who had patronised the café since its opening in 1884. Leon, his nose analysing every single molecule in the air, approved enthusiastically. This was a place that knew what food was all about.

The man looked carefully around until he spotted an empty table next to the large windows facing Národní Street and the magnificent façade of the National Theatre.

"Awesome," ahhed Dora, clasping her hands.

The less emotional Etta was about to remove her coat when

Dora reminded her with a frown that they were only wearing their pyjamas underneath. Impatient to cut through all the small talk and get straight down to business, Etta had to wait as an unsmiling waiter brought the menus and took their drinks order. Two cappuccinos and a coffee.

"You should try the Slavia sausages," suggested Janda. "They're made by a celebrated Prague butcher. And Slavia's eggs Benedict is a must-eat…"

"Eggs Benedict doesn't sound very Czech."

"True, but it's that good."

"I think I'll go for the yogurt and walnut granola with cinnamon," said Etta, determined to stick to the bargain basement items on the menu. Leon, lying on the floor, wriggled impatiently.

"I'll try the sausages," said Dora.

"But we never eat sausages for breakfast," cried Etta, feeling betrayed.

"But we've never eaten breakfast in a Czech café…"

When the waiter came back with eggs Benedict, cheese and Prague ham for Josef Janda, the sausages for Dora, and a plain cup of yogurt for her, Etta wished she had ordered eggs and bacon. The most delicious scent of waffles completely overwhelmed the weak aroma of cinnamon coming from her yogurt. And things got even worse when the waiter came back with a bowl of scrambled eggs and a slice of bacon for Leon.

"This is from our chef, he used to have a Basset who lived with him for 14 years." Etta was going to protest, but the waiter, still deadly serious, added, "He said he took care to make it a light dish; he used no butter in the eggs, and the bacon is just a little golden slice. There's cubes of toasted wholegrain bread on the side so he will have the energy for plenty of long walks today."

Leon was sitting in front of the waiter, his eyes droopy and languid, as they became whenever he needed to steal someone's heart, his tail swishing the air in agreement with the man's every word.

"Thanks so much, we'll say hello to the chef as soon as we've finished," said Dora. Etta felt injustice was, as usual, prevailing.

"Mr Janda, we left the theatre's bar around 11pm. Did you stay much longer?" she asked as Dora eyed her disapprovingly.

"Indeed. It was a good gathering, and when the theatre closed at midnight, we carried on in a nearby pub. It was an excellent night."

"Who were you with?" Etta asked him. While eating a spoonful of healthy fresh fruit mixed in with her yogurt, she was eyeing the rich eggs in Mr Janda's dish.

"Are you sure you don't want to try some?" he asked kindly.

"No, they're very bad for one's cholesterol."

"Such a pity. You have high cholesterol?"

"I don't have high cholesterol, but I do take positive steps to prevent it."

"Very wise of you," he said, biting into a large chunk of bread with ham and cheese and sending Etta a blissful look.

"The sausages are delicious, Mr Janda, thanks for the suggestion. I will make sure I walk my 10,000 steps today so that cholesterol won't trouble me either…"

"What were you saying about the pub?" Etta cut across the two partners in crime and their talk of delicious food.

"Oh yes, we all went: Mike Smolak, Egon Zima and Eva Kladivova. I'm not too sure if you know them all?"

"We were introduced, yes. And did you stay there for long?"

"Oh yes, we Czechs have an awful habit when it comes to drinking. Once we get started, we find it hard to stop, especially if we're with people we haven't seen in a long while. It was gone 2am before I got back to my hotel."

"Did Ms Kladivova call a taxi?"

"No, she said her hotel was just the other side of the bridge," he said, his head pointing in the direction he meant.

"No one offered to accompany her?"

"No, we just walked with her to the Most Legii and left her at this end of the bridge…"

"Wouldn't it have been safer to escort her all the way to the hotel?"

"Safer?"

"Well, you know, it's never good for a woman to be walking about alone at night…"

"But we're in Prague," the man said, disconcerted. "Anyone's safe alone, especially in the centre. Apart from the occasional pickpockets – who mainly prey on crowds of tourists – there is virtually no crime in Prague."

"It looks like you're totally wrong there. You clearly haven't heard the news."

"What news?"

"Eva Kladivova was found dead early this morning."

"What are you saying?" Janda said, lowering his fork with his last bite of Prague ham on it back into the dish.

"She was stabbed and thrown in the Vltava River last night. Or rather, from what you've just said, early this morning."

"How… how… do you know?"

Dora frowned at her friend again. Etta should have left the man to finish his breakfast before telling him.

"We went out first thing this morning and saw the police recovering a body from the river. We saw the body was dressed in a long red robe that I thought I recognised as Ms Kladivova's. When I mentioned that to the police, we were asked to identify the body. It was indeed Eva Kladivova, beyond any possible doubt."

"Oh my goodness! Why didn't you tell me sooner?" The man seemed genuinely shocked.

"We weren't sure how involved you might be…"

"Involved?"

"Yes, involved. What did you do after you left her? Did you stick with the other men?"

"Not really. We are each staying in a different hotel, so we simply parted at the bridge and made our way to our own accommodation."

"And where's your hotel?"

"Further up along Národní Street." He signalled to Dora that he would like to borrow her map and showed them a point about 200 metres away from the café.

"So you all parted and you walked straight back to your hotel. Or did you stop on the way?"

"No, I didn't. But what do the police say? Who attacked her?"

"The police did not tell us anything."

"It must have been a robbery that got out of hand. Eva Kladivova was the wrong woman to pick on..."

"The wrong woman?" Etta frowned.

"She wasn't the kind who'd just hand over her purse or jewels; she would fight and scream to draw attention."

"I don't think so," Etta replied drily. "Usually if an assailant is confronted by a recalcitrant victim, they would engage in a fight and he would surely attack the front of her body. But Eva Kladivova was stabbed in the back... No, in my opinion, that doesn't fit with your theory of a robbery gone wrong."

"You mean she might have been killed on purpose?"

"I'm not a police officer, nor a private investigator, but that's how I see it. How well did you know her?"

"We've been competitors for what seems like a lifetime," he murmured. Etta looked at him, as if to encourage him to tell her more. "We were in the same B2B industry, selling electrical components mostly to companies in the United States. That's why we both attended the meeting after the concert last night. We started in business after the Velvet Revolution, when companies had to accept the challenge of privatisation."

"That was surely a good thing," suggested Etta, "the end of Communism and dictatorship."

"Absolutely, but at the same time, when you're used to working in a controlled regime, the transition to a liberal economy with cutthroat competition does not come easy..."

"Cutthroat, eh?"

"Tough," the man corrected himself, blushing. "Just tough competition. Up until then, companies had all been state owned. They knew what they were going to sell in advance, they knew what they were going to earn. It didn't matter how good you were at business, nor how good your product was, and there was no need for marketing. People's lives were stable: they knew they were going to keep their jobs for a lifetime, their flats were paid for, they'd have retirement schemes to support them throughout their old age..."

"Sounds like heaven in these troubled times of ours," Etta said ironically.

"Well, it came at a high price. We had no freedom of thought or expression; what we could buy or eat was limited to what the Government thought we might need. And that 'stability' was undermined by the fact that if your neighbour took a dislike to you, they could ruin you for the most mundane of reasons. It was simple to tell the police you'd said something against the Government, and then you would disappear overnight. Yes, that 'stability' came at a high price, but still, when the free market arrived, I confess we were not ready... not at all."

"You said your company went into competition with Ms Eva Kladivova's?"

"Indeed, and she is... sorry, was a strong rival. I confess, I could never adopt the Capitalist mentality completely. Mind you, I very much embrace the current system vs the old one. But I could never understand the need to exploit workers; I believe in every company, there should be more of a balance between what the managers and owners earn and what the workers get. I'm not a Communist, but neither am I an uncompromising Capitalist..."

"The happy middle ground," whispered Dora.

"That's correct. And each of us, every individual has the duty and responsibility to find that happy middle ground..."

"I take it Ms Kladivova's middle ground was different from yours?"

"She was very ambitious. She managed to change her life completely, going from being an ordinary person to a wealthy one."

"And later, you'll be attending... what was it? A conference of some sort?"

"The concert last night was the opening event for the US Embassy and the Department of Commerce's conference and roadshow to facilitate commercial relationships between the United States and the Czech Republic. I know Mike of old; we kept in touch when he moved to the US. On this occasion, I want him to help us find new US clients who would appreciate our products."

"Ms Eva Kladivova was determined to win the same kind of attention for her business, I guess."

"That's right, and Egon Zima, too. It was a business event last night to all intents and purposes. But the fact that Mike Smolak is not only Czech himself, but also an old acquaintance made the whole atmosphere rather more relaxed and informal."

"You mean you all knew each other?"

"Indeed we did, since the times leading up to the Velvet Revolution when we all gravitated towards the US Embassy in Prague. I'll be honest with you in a way I could never have been back then – we were all supporting dissident groups. We were not really involved on the frontline, but we did our part to help dissident students and intellectuals with little favours such as sending information abroad, making photocopies of their material..."

"And you *all* knew each other back then?"

"No, actually, I can't remember Eva Kladivova from that time, but Mike used to work for the US Embassy, and Egon and I met with him and the Ambassador quite regularly. We were considered sympathisers of the new movement by the Embassy, but in the eyes of the Czech police, we were attending the

Embassy as business managers at a time when the government was trying to open up to international trade. By the way, I saw you talking to Marketa last night. She worked at the Embassy as a nurse, but I'm sure she was doing her fair share for the Revolution, too."

"So when did you meet Ms Kladivova?"

"We've met at a few industry events in recent years; we were never close, but we got on well…"

Liar! Etta thought, remembering the hatred she'd seen on Eva's face the previous night. Pretending indifference, she continued her interview.

"Is Mr Egon Zima in the same line of business as you are?"

"No, no, he's in the textile industry. We are not in competition – well, our companies aren't, at least, but he too wanted to have a chance to speak to Mike Smolak last night. And he knew Eva Kladivova, too."

"How do you know that?"

"There was a degree of familiarity between them, although they didn't seem to be on the best of terms. There was some sort of conflict going on between the two of them last night – or at least, that's how it seemed to me. I might be wrong."

Was he trying to switch suspicion on to another fellow? Whether she liked it or not, Etta had become involved in a series of murder investigations since she and Dora had become close friends in Castelmezzano the previous year, and had found she had a natural talent for sleuthing, so she made a mental note of Josef's words, and her doubts about him. She would not allow his comments, or those of anyone else, to bias her thinking; she would simply take note of what each of them had to say, and only when she had heard enough would she decide if they were just opinions, critical observations, leads or astute attempts to send her investigations down the wrong path.

Dora was looking up at her, touching her nose with her left hand as if she was wondering how to piece together the information she had just heard. But the real bad news arrived at the end of their meal, when all their plates had been cleared and the waiter brought over the bill.

Josef Janda paid for all three of them before the two women could even look for their purses.

"Mr Janda, that's very nice of you, but you didn't have to..."

"Don't you worry, I can always claim it against my taxes," he winked at them. "But mostly, it's because it's been my pleasure to talk to you."

"Will you be going back to your hotel?"

He looked at his watch. "Not now. I have a little time before the conference starts, and I'd rather have a walk after what you've just told me. Poor Eva. I also need to phone Mrs Coleman – surely the police will want to speak with the people who last saw Eva, so I'll tell her that I went drinking with her. Yes, I need a little time alone..."

And he left, walking towards the south side of the Vltava River.

～

Leon was determined to walk on the right-hand side of the Vltava, continually sniffing his imaginary trail, much as he had done on the left bank. Not only did he forget to mark every single tree along his route, not only did he ignore all the other dogs passing by, he also didn't stop whenever the two women wanted to pause. Past the Gothic Kranner's fountain they went, not even hesitating to observe the workers preparing river activities like pedal boats and the colourful zorbing balloons inside which people could float on the water. But when they arrived by the wooden rails that worked as icebreakers during the winter season, and the view from under the linden trees opened up across to the beautiful neo-Renaissance Smetana Building with its Sgraffito drawings and the willow tree embracing the bronze statue of the composer with its flowing branches, Dora had to insist the Basset halt his maddening rush.

"Just take a pause and have a look around, Leon," she told him as severely as she could, which did not amount to much. Her eyes lingered on the contrast between the ochre Smetana, shining as if made of gold, and the white building beside it, with its solid watch tower topped by one of the hundreds of greeny-blue copper spires that decorated the city. The Charles Bridge stood in all its glory before the carpet of red roofs and spires leading all the way up to the St Vitus Cathedral, surrounded by the white walls of impressive Renaissance buildings. The façade of the Liechtenstein Palace was reflected in the waters of the Vltava, so close to where they'd seen Eva's body earlier that morning. Now, in the glory of this hour, with the Petřín Hill in the background shining in the bright green of a gorgeous spring day, it all seemed like a bad dream.

It was no good. Dora could not face so much beauty all at once and remain unmoved. As she clasped her hands, she let Leon's leash slip, and before Etta could react, the hound, wondering what all the fuss and oohs and wows were about, was back on his trail. The metal part of the leash hitting the cobbled street with a rhythmic tang as he trotted on, ignoring the panoramic Novotného footbridge Dora had so badly wanted to see, he headed directly towards the Charles Bridge along the narrow pavement of Křížovnická Street where cars, scooters and trams raced each other as if competing in a rally, the two horrified women panting behind.

5

MR MIKE SMOLAK

I t was always a mystery to Etta how such a short-legged train-like dog could manage to run as fast as Leon. Certainly, she was no Carl Lewis, but neither was Leon. Still, neither she nor Dora could catch up with him. The hound would glance over his shoulder every now and then, just to make sure he'd not put too much distance between himself and his bipeds, nor too little, then his sturdy legs would carry on with their one-dog race.

Leon's reasoning wasn't at all skewed, in his humble opinion. Left to their own devices, these two women would never get anywhere; they spent most of their time idly gazing around, and he was starting to dread crossing Charles Bridge. Every time, they stood there for ages, or moved from the left side to the right 'taking in views', stopping at some strange statues – and we're not talking one or two, but thirty of them; he had counted them. And most annoyingly of all, forbidding Leon to pee against them. Now what's the point of admiring anything taller than yourself if you cannot leave your signature on it?

Humans are strange creatures, he concluded. *They demand plenty of hard work from this poor, exhausted beastie.* Still, he had adopted them and was responsible for their wellbeing, so he'd continue to make sure they all lived a happy life together.

Only once he reached the other end of the now not-so-empty bridge, just in front of the steps going down to Kampa island, did Leon stop his trotting. Etta and Dora were still following behind, the danger of them stopping on the bridge for hours seemingly over, at least for now. But would the women allow him to go back to the park or would they take him home?

Sniffing the threat of a refusal, Leon waited for the women to get just a little closer before taking the steps down.

"Stop! Wretched hushpuppy, stop, I said!" Etta cried from behind.

But the dog took exactly the same route as he had followed earlier that morning, halting only when he got to where the police were still investigating and faced a man who was talking to Lieutenant Baloun.

∾

When Etta and Dora arrived, they were really not a pretty sight: sweaty red faces, ruffled hair and out of breath, but unable to undo their coats in case they revealed the pyjamas underneath. It took them a while to get their breath back, while the Lieutenant observed them with a wry smile.

"So, you're back."

"*He* is back." Etta nodded towards Leon. "We merely followed him." She did not like the note of sarcasm in the Lieutenant's voice. Was he alluding to the fact that killers are rumoured always to return to the scene of the crime? Could the Lieutenant seriously be implying that she and Dora might be guilty of such a crime? Or was he joking again?

In the meantime, this human's worst friend had positioned himself beside the man facing the Lieutenant. It was only when he raised his head after having patted the dog that Etta and Dora recognised him as Mike Smolak.

"Good morning," he said with a smile, "I didn't know you had such a lovely companion." Leon was still busy sniffing the man and saying hello to him, flogging Smolak's leg with his tail as if there were no tomorrow.

"Lovely companion, my eye!" growled Etta. Grabbing Leon's leash, she addressed the dog. "You're such a monster!"

Leon melted on to the ground, his body growing longer than ever, rubbing his nose with his paws in a demonstration of shame. It'd take a heart of stone to resist his pleas for forgiveness.

"OK, I'm not going to roast you this time," Etta conceded.

"Poor little one," said Dora, as always taking Leon's side. "Maybe he was frightened by all the traffic on the road and the crowds of people on the bridge."

"Frightened? He was having fun!"

"Bassets are notorious for having to have everything their own way," said Mr Smolak. "Even when they're seeming to comply with your wishes..."

"You're almost correct, except Leon does not so much as pretend to be complying with our wishes."

"Do you have a Basset back home?" asked Dora.

"I don't, but my neighbours do, so I know their ways well." While speaking, he gently scratched Leon below his ear, something the hound simply loved.

"The body has been taken away?" Etta asked Baloun.

"Yes, it would have been hard to keep the tourists away from it otherwise," said the Lieutenant, pointing to the area ahead of them that was still cordoned off. "At least this way, the forensics can do their job without much interference."

"Gosh, I'd almost forgotten," said Etta, opening her handbag and taking out a poo bag. The Lieutenant looked at her in horror as she pushed it towards him; Smolak's blue eyes lit up with a twinkle of humour.

"Are you looking for a bin?" the Lieutenant asked, pulling his hand away from the unwanted gift.

"No, it's not... *that*," Etta protested. Did he really think she would be trying to press dog poo into the hands of a police officer? "We walked up to the Legion Bridge and we found this lipstick compact. It might mean nothing, but the lipstick is a vibrant red that matches the victim's dress. I wondered if that could be where the woman was killed and thrown into the river, and the currents carried her body here. Of course, I did not want to mess any evidence up with my fingerprints, but all I had with me was Leon's poo bags. Clean ones, I mean."

"So you haven't touched the case?"

"No, I picked it up using the bag."

The Lieutenant did not say anything for a while. He was looking at the Legion Bridge, then he unfolded the bag and had a look at both the lipstick and the case through the plastic.

"Where exactly did you find it?"

Etta showed him the couple of photos she had taken of the place. "And I marked the exact spot with chalk," she said, pointing to a circle and cross she had drawn on the bridge.

"Do you normally carry chalk in your bag?" Mr Smolak asked.

"No, but there were plenty of little stones around, so I used one of the whiter ones and it worked."

"I'll send the forensics to have a look. I am not sure the lipstick belonged to Ms Kladivova, but it could be that the woman was thrown in the river from that bridge, and that the case slipped out of her bag. Which we haven't found yet, by the way."

"Yes, the woman could easily have been thrown into the Vltava from that bridge, especially since her hotel was on the other side of it and she was crossing it alone. You had left her somewhere near the end of the bridge, hadn't you, Mr Smolak?"

Mike Smolak let out a whistle of surprise, then nodded to confirm what Etta had said.

"Her real name is Jessica Fletcher," the Lieutenant explained. "She's visiting Prague incognito. So, Mr Smolak, if you've done anything wrong, you should know there's no way out for you."

"I see I'm in a terrible position. Am I the only suspect?"

"No, you're in good company," Etta replied nonchalantly. "There are at least two others, Egon Zima and Josef Janda, plus anyone else who was at the theatre last night and may have kept an eye on your movements, waiting for the right moment to strike."

The Lieutenant was recording what Etta was saying in his notebook. Mr Smolak asked him a question.

"Are these ladies ahead of you in the investigation?"

"In a way – the lipstick compact is a point for them, but I might have an ace up my sleeve. After all, I am a police officer. But I see I'm going to have my work cut out, stopping them from snooping. Are you heading to the Embassy, Mr Smolak?"

"Yes, I have an appointment with the Ambassador before going on to the conference site."

"Can I ask you to find the time to come to the police station early this afternoon with a list of all the people who attended the concert at the theatre last night?"

"Yes, I will ask the Secretary at the Embassy to email you the list straight away, and I'll come by around 3pm."

After the Lieutenant had nodded his consent, Mr Smolak addressed the two women.

"Ladies, are you planning to walk to the park?"

"No, we're heading back home now for a little rest and to plan our day," said Dora.

"If the Lieutenant no longer needs us," added Etta, curious enough to stay put in her pyjamas if need be.

"No, you're free to go. And listen – it's been a pleasure joking with you, but things can get rough in a murder investigation. Please be careful and don't go snooping."

"Of course not," said Dora. "We're just tourists."

Etta tried to make her expression as angelic and innocent as Dora's. The Lieutenant shook his head and waved them away.

"Where's home?" Mr Smolak asked them.

"A little street behind Malostranské náměstí."

"You're not taking Mostecká Street, are you?"

"That's the route we've used so far. It seems to be the straightest route to and from the bridge."

"The straightest in Prague does not necessarily mean the quickest. You need to learn how to avoid the tourist crowds; it's a survival skill here. Come along."

From Na Kampě square, the branches of the linden trees crossing to form a shady tunnel, Mr Smolak took them down a little street winding in between the magnificent palaces of Prague. Even in this street, the pavements were cobbled with tiny flat stones, forming an elegant pattern of chequered squares set beneath ancient cast-iron lamps hanging from the walls. Then completely unexpectedly, they found themselves on a tiny bridge on the Čertovka Canal – also called the Devil's Stream – overlooking a watermill wheel. A little gremlin was sitting stretching his legs over the water just beyond the wheel, as if he was making fun of the poor miller working hard to earn his bread.

Mr Smolak stopped just long enough to allow them to have a proper look.

"Come along, there's always more to see in this city." His steps were the long and loping strides of a person confident about managing their hours – never hurried, but always on time.

On their right was a thick copse of trees, and before them stood a long wall covered with brightly coloured graffiti that women with prams, young adults and tourists were eyeing curiously.

"The Lennon wall," cried Dora in surprise. She had read all about this wall commemorating the singer John Lennon with graffiti and lyrics since his death in 1980, which had also become a symbol of freedom of speech. Nowadays, it visually discussed global issues, from climate change to standing up against dictatorial regimes around the world. She had not realised the wall would be so close to their temporary home.

"That's it. I see you've prepared well for your visit. As it's not far from where you're staying, you can come back and look at it any time. Will you be staying in Prague for long?"

"About three weeks," said Dora proudly. "I hope it will be enough time to discover the city's treasures."

"And secrets," added Etta.

A blonde woman interrupted and asked if she could pat Leon. Dora stopped and Leon looked up at the young woman with dreamy eyes. She was such a cutie.

"My own Basset, Augustine, is waiting for me back in Australia. Mum and Dad are taking care of her. I'm loving my trip to Europe, but I miss her so much. Would you mind if I took a picture with... what's this beauty's name?"

"Leon," replied Dora. "Of course we don't mind."

Leon took his job as a dog model seriously. He knew that after taking their pictures, people would praise him for being so photogenic. Whatever the word meant, it sounded good, and Leon was fond of compliments and adulation of any sort. This time was no different. Set against the backdrop of the Lennon wall, the picture delighted the young woman, who was so overjoyed, she landed a big kiss on his head.

"You're such a lovely, gorgeous Basset Hound, I'd love to take you home."

"I love you too," Leon's dreamy eyes seemed to reply. "But I've got those two to take care of. Goodbye, my one true love." And they parted, the poor dog broken hearted.

"I see it's a good job you're staying a while," said Smolak, the same humour Etta had noticed earlier again lighting up his eyes. "Leon's fans must slow your visits down considerably."

Dora laughed. "Actually, they provide us with a good excuse to pause and catch our breath every now and again."

"Have you always lived in the US?" Etta asked Smolak as they passed yet another pretty church, a porch standing between its two towers with a couple of dark Gothic arches leading to a cloister.

"This is the church of Saint Mary under the Chain. It belongs to the Knights of Malta... but you were asking me about the States. I was actually born and bred in the Czech Republic, or Czechoslovakia as it was in those times, then as a young man, I started working with the US Embassy. They must have liked me as after the Velvet Revolution, they offered me a job. Not at the Embassy, I'm not much of a diplomat, but I had been working with the Trade Office and they offered me a place within the US Department of Commerce."

"Do you like your life in the States?" enquired Dora.

"Absolutely. I don't think I would have had so many chances to grow my career here in Prague, but I'm always happy to be back."

"Which must happen quite often, I guess."

"Not that often. At times, it can be three to four years before I return."

"So," Etta remarked so vigorously that she failed in her attempt to sound casual, "you already knew many of the company owners and managers present at the meeting yesterday?"

"I know quite a few of them, but not all by any means. I certainly know Josef Janda and Egon Zima well from our Embassy days, and I had spoken to Eva Kladivova on the phone and corresponded with her via email on a number of occasions, but I had never met her in person until last night."

"But she's been in business since the Velvet Revolution, from what I've heard..."

"That's correct, but she was a force of nature. She would not wait for the Embassy Trade Office to instigate a relationship between hers and companies in the United States; she found the way to make a move on her own. When she did get in touch, it was with specific requests. I certainly knew about her company, it was..." He broke off, looking embarrassed now, as if he was finding it difficult to think of the right words to use in the circumstances. "It was a pleasure to meet her finally, even if our acquaintance didn't last too long." He paused again. "You know, crime is not really in the nature of the Czech people. I can't imagine what happened last night; it's so rare for someone to get killed here, and in the city centre..."

"Yesterday, you were drinking together. Did you notice anything unusual in Ms Kladivova's demeanour?"

The man shook his head, a soft smile flashing on to his face. "Now I see what Lieutenant Baloun meant. You're back into your Fletcher role, aren't you?"

Etta was starting to get irritated by the comparison. Not only was she not a writer – such a sloppy, melancholic lot – but also, how old had Angela Lansbury been when the movies were shot? Did she, Etta, really look that old? She had always been convinced she looked at least ten years younger than she was, so why weren't these men comparing her with Alice Nevers, Jane Rizzoli or another of those sassy women detectives? But before she could vent her spleen, the man continued.

"To answer your question, no, I did not see anything strange in anyone's demeanour. Even the divorcees seemed to be at ease with each other... a little sarcastic, maybe, and Ms Kladivova looked him up and down with a sneer a couple of times, but I imagine that's only to be expected..."

"Divorcees?"

"Yes, Egon Zima and Eva Kladivova were once married. They divorced a few years ago. Did you not know?"

"No, Mr Janda didn't mention it."

"He's such a discreet man..."

"Are you sure he even knew?"

"Yes, I'm sure. After all, Eva Kladivova was his main competitor, so he would know everything about her."

They walked on in silence for a while, Etta taking in this new piece of information.

"Are you going to speak to Mr Zima?" Smolak asked.

"Why? Should we?" Etta was on the defensive.

"I thought you were investigating the murder," the man said, his eyes twinkling.

"Not really, we just happened to bump into you and Mr Janda."

"I beg your pardon if I misunderstood your interest in the matter. I simply thought you had a plan."

"No, we don't."

"We're going to meet up with Marketa, the former Embassy Nurse, at some point," Dora said, "so she can show us around Prague."

"Dear Marketa, I see," but the man looked disappointed. "So you are just a couple of tourists after all." He stopped. "I'm turning left for the Embassy here, so if you walk straight on, you'll find yourself in Malostranské náměstí. That is, unless you want to have a look at the US Embassy. It's housed in the Schönborn Palace, which is certainly one of Prague's beauties..."

"Is it far from here?"

"About 200 metres, I'd say."

"Then yes, we'd like that."

"I won't be able to take you in, but as friends of Christine's, you could ask to be invited for a visit. It's a gorgeous place with a splendid garden."

"Yes," confirmed Dora, "Christine offered to invite us to visit the Embassy, and we'll take her up on that as soon as the conference is over. I imagine she's very busy at the moment."

They arrived in front of an imposing white building with soft pink shades, decorated windows and a large wooden door enclosed by two marble columns and topped by a balcony on which the American flag waved. Security officers stood by a smaller door which allowed visitors in.

"When you visit, don't forget to see the Embassy Park and the Gloriette."

"A park?" asked Dora in surprise. They were standing amongst palatial houses on a cobbled street, the castle towering over them; she could hardly imagine a park anywhere.

"I'll tell you a secret," Mr Smolak said. "If you walk straight along Vlašská Street, you'll have access to the Petřín Park, which covers a large area behind us all the way to the Strahov Monastery, and walking south you'll get to the Hunger Wall. Prague is such a green city, you will wonder whether you're in a city at all, or in some vineyard in Tuscany."

"And this park must be closer to home than Kampa," said Dora, happy to have more space in the neighbourhood for the hound.

"Kampa's are nice gardens, but this is a real park with plenty of wilderness. But I must go. As much as I'd love to be your guide, duty calls." He stopped to pluck a card from his wallet and handed it to Etta. "Feel free to call me if you need me or... want to question me further." He winked at them before being checked over by security and disappearing inside the Embassy.

6

MR EGON ZIMA

"If it was not a robbery, then he is the killer," murmured Etta as soon as Mike Smolak had vanished from view.

"Oh, Etta, no! He's too nice."

"I don't call that nice," replied Etta. "Cheeky is the appropriate word."

"Like the Lieutenant…"

"Do you think it's a national trait?"

"Yes, it is. I read in some of our guides that Czech people have a wicked sense of humour. It must have helped them to deal with all they had to put up with in their darker years."

As they talked, Leon was pulling them silently along Vlašská Street.

"Where are we going?" asked Etta, startled. "Aren't we meant to be heading home?"

"Goodness," said Dora as if waking from a dream, but for once, she was holding on to the leash firmly. "Leon, where do you think you're going?"

The dog only turned his head and sighed, his body still pointing like a compass needle in the direction he intended to go.

"Do you think he overheard Mr Smolak talking about the park?" asked Dora.

"Of course not, but I'm sure he can smell 'greenery' of any kind, and probably happy dogs."

"Come on, Leon," said Dora. "Let's go back home. We will soon go out again, I know how curious you are."

The dog did not even pause. On such a gorgeous day, why would anyone want to go back inside? Especially when things were working out so nicely.

"I'll take him," said Etta impatiently, snatching the leash from Dora's hands. "He needs to learn when not to put up a fight he cannot win." As she spoke, she got closer to the dog and pulled him in the direction she wanted to go. In response, Leon sat down. Etta pulled harder; Leon lay down on the ground, paws spread apart, playing dead.

"OK then, you stay here, but we're going home to get some nice food. Some snacks and biscuits." Etta dropped the leash, turned towards Dora and slid her arm under her friend's. As unwilling as the other woman was to leave the poor Basset all alone in the street, she followed Etta.

This is most unexpected, Leon thought. Generally, Etta would drag and howl and grump until she realised she had no choice but to let him win the game. Now, he was puzzled – were they really going back home and leaving him all alone? Without anyone protecting them? Could he let them go undefended?

Before they were even 10 metres away from him, he sprang up to follow them. Etta caught the leash and home they went.

∼

As they faced Malostranské náměstí, now heaving with traffic and people, Dora had a good look around. Every time they passed by, she wanted to become more intimately acquainted with each of the Renaissance and Baroque buildings, now noting the detail on their gables – so refined, almost like lacework – now taking in the fresco of a Madonna on one of the façades, now exploring the statues decorating the balconies. Her gaze wandering up on high, she literally bumped into a passer-by.

"I'm so sorry," she cried as she tried hard not to lose her balance.

"You should be more careful," the man snapped, doing nothing to help.

"Woof!" Leon protested. He was aware how distracted his roundish lady could be, but that was no reason for anyone, except Leon himself, to reproach her.

"I'm OK, Leon," she tried to calm him. Then, as soon as she had recovered her stability, she looked at the passer-by more carefully. "Is that you, Mr Zima?"

The man looked surprised she should know him.

"That's my name, yes…"

"We met yesterday at the National Theatre, you were talking to Marketa. I'm Dora Pepe, Christine Coleman's friend."

The man, who looked even more dishevelled this morning, finally seemed to place her. He greeted her with a nod, but did not speak.

"I guess you're going to the conference, aren't you?"

"Er… indeed, I am."

Etta joined them. In her eagerness to get back home, she had not realised Dora and Leon had fallen behind, and she had turned only when she heard a familiar bark.

"Good morning," she said.

"This is my friend, Etta Passolina. I'm sure you remember her from last night, too…"

"Sure, sure, but now, I'm afraid, I need to go."

"Are you heading for the conference?" asked Etta before the man could run away.

"I am, and I'm a little late…"

"Don't you worry about that. Have you heard the terrible news?"

"The terrible news?" the man repeated blankly.

Dora frowned at her friend. Surely Etta wouldn't be brutal

with the poor man, the ex-husband of the deceased. But brutal she was.

"Well, I am sorry to be the one to break the news, but Ms Eva Kladivova was murdered last night."

"Oh that. Yes, I know," he said, as if it was an everyday occurrence, hearing that his former wife had been killed.

"How do you know?"

The man paused before answering. "Christine Coleman called me and informed me."

"As you were one of the last people to see her, I'm sure the police will be wanting to speak to you."

"That's none of your business!"

"I was just going to let you know we've already spoken to them, first thing this morning."

"I see." The man seemed to recognise that he had overreacted. "But now, I really must go. Have a good day."

"And the same to you," Etta said, whilst Dora waved her hand as if he were a little kid. As the man moved down the square, the two women stood still for a while, each perplexed for her own reasons.

"Now what do you make of that?" Etta asked.

"He must be upset. After all, Eva was once his wife…"

"But I found his reaction peculiar to say the least, and unconvincing…"

"We all react differently to pain."

"So you think it's rational behaviour for him to be heading to the conference as if nothing's happened?"

"But he isn't heading to the conference," said Dora, who had been following the man's progress. "He's turned left – the Embassy and the conference site are on the right."

"Well done, Miss Pepe," said Etta, looking towards the point Dora indicated. "He's gone on to Mostecká Street, which is hardly surprising."

"What do you mean?"

"Don't killers always return to the scene of the crime?"

7

MISS MARKETA CIPROVA

After a quiet Sunday spent behaving like perfect tourists, Etta, Dora and Leon were ready to see more of the sights of Prague. But on Nerudova Street, they felt as if they'd joined a river of people, all moving in the same direction up towards Prague Castle. Dora had brought her guide with her and she patiently pointed out all the most important places as well as the intriguing house signs that distinguished one address from another before plain street numbers came into fashion, until even she had to acknowledge it was just too crowded to stop in the middle of the street. The pavements were wide, but they were partly occupied by bar tables and chairs, their occupants enjoying the sun and viewing the slowly moving crowd as if it was a herd of sheep, or maybe slightly more exotic animals.

Then, the herd turned onto a narrow street to the right. It was impossible to stop to take in the view, especially as Etta and Dora were busy trying to protect Leon, who was barely visible among the legs surrounding him. Finally, the tight passageway opened up and the two women found themselves in such a large, open space, they could barely call it a square.

They were facing the wrought-iron gates of Prague Castle, a huge, imposing building. The river of people flowed sluggishly in that direction, while Etta, Dora and Leon took refuge on the western side of the square, searching for the less busy Kanovnická Street that would take them out of the madding crowd and back to what they had come to view as small-town Prague.

Looking towards the greenery of the Castle Gardens, Dora gave a shriek. "Here it is, Nový Svět! Where Marketa lives."

"It looks like we're back in Český Krumlov," said Etta, gazing at the little paved road with a stone wall on one side and tiny enchanting buildings on the other that so much reminded her of their first stop in the Czech Republic just a few days earlier.

"True, Prague seems to be so many places at once. I wasn't expecting to find such peace so close to the castle."

Leon too felt better now that no one was threatening to tread on his paws.

The little street was actually much longer than Dora and Etta had anticipated. In fact, it stretched so far that they finally realised they should have asked Marketa for the number of her house.

"We can't exactly check each door, hoping to find the owner's name," muttered Etta.

"How about asking at the café we just passed, maybe they know Marketa. It looks like a neighbourhood where people know each other."

The café was cosy, with dark oak floors and ancient furniture inside. Outside, a few tables were arranged on the pavement. A blonde woman with a huge smile on lips coated heavily in pink lipstick welcomed them. At first, she was a little reluctant to give away personal information about Marketa, but once Dora had reassured her that they were friends wishing to visit the nurse, she opened up.

"Marketa lives in the house with the lamb sign by the door. Just walk down the road another block and it's on your left; you can't miss it."

Feeling eyes on the back of her neck, Etta turned and spotted an old man sitting at a table for one near the door. He had sunken cheeks and two deep brown eyes that flared up with a malicious twinkle as they met Etta's before going back to pretending to read the newspaper in his hands.

The two friends went out onto the street, stopping at a little wooden door in a two-storey ochre building, a golden lamb on its arch identifying it as the nurse's home.

"This is it," said Dora with conviction, ringing the bell.

Marketa opened the door, her cheeks pink, her eyes bright, her conversation rapid, confirming their first impression of her: this woman was always busy doing something.

"There you are! You made it! I hope it wasn't too difficult to find me; it's such a tiny road that most people miss it."

"Actually, we were about to walk towards the castle gardens; we only just noticed the fork. And it's so peaceful here."

"That's why I love it. It's not too great for shopping, but we residents manage to organise things, and we've got the benefit of being close to everything else – the parks, Malá Strana and the Old Town – without being devoured by tourists."

"I thought I saw a couple of B&Bs along the way..."

"True, you did, but you see, I don't dislike tourists at all... in small numbers. The few who stay down here are nice, respectful people who appreciate the peace of the place. I often meet them in one of the two cafés we have in the street, and they tell me they like being able to mix with the local folks."

"Have you heard any more news about Eva Kladivova's death?" Etta asked.

"No, the newspapers only mentioned where she had been found, which I of course knew already thanks to the message you sent on Saturday. No hints as to the reason why she might have been killed, the poor woman. But I'm chatting instead of inviting you in."

It was then that Marketa spotted Leon.

"And who is this beauty?" she said, bending down to allow the dog to smell her hand. Having given her a good sniff, he was happy to be gently patted and complimented. "Is this the Leon you had to get back to on Friday night?"

"Yes, this is Leon, our canine companion on our trips. And, indeed, when we are at home."

"You're so lucky to have such a lovely companion, I'm sure he takes good care of you. But please, do come in."

They entered a charming living room with a low barrel-vault ceiling, oak floors and cream coloured walls, a little fireplace in a corner, a white framed window surrounded by a painted green border and plenty of potted plants on the windowsills and bookshelves. A stool close to the bookcase, scissors and a watering can paid testament to the activity occupying the woman that morning. On a large chest of drawers and scattered over other pieces of furniture in the room was a large collection of framed photographs: portraits of children, weddings, elderly people, groups.

"I'm not married, but I have assisted plenty of people," the nurse explained. "And some of them have become like family to me, which is good because should I need anything, I can just ring one of them."

"Don't you have any family at all? Brothers or sisters, I mean?"

"No, I was an only child and my parents are no longer with us. But I have family in Karlštejn, two cousins of mine live there and we see each other quite regularly. Either I go to them to enjoy the countryside, or they come to me when they need a city fix. But before I take out all my photo albums and we chatter our way through old memories, how about a cup of coffee or tea?"

The two Italian friends promptly asked for tea. When Marketa returned, she was holding a large tray with a teapot and porcelain cups, decorated with a design of chickens in the countryside, and a selection of biscuits.

"I can't bake, but my cousin is a kitchen queen. In fact, she works at Karlštejn Castle. Not in the café, though, which is a shame; she gives guided tours…"

Leon looked at her with eyes like melting chocolate.

"I guess sugar is no good for him, but I made him a little toast with Prague ham and cheese. Is that OK?"

Leon looked at Etta and Dora, afraid they might say no for some obscure reason.

"It's just a little slice of ham, I'm sure he will appreciate it," added Marketa. This woman, Leon decided, was a friend for life. Etta and Dora, reassured that the snack wasn't going to be too large or heavy, said yes, and his new best friend laid a porcelain dish on the floor, the toast broken into bite-size pieces. As he ate, Leon pondered on how he could move to Prague and live a happy life; there were plenty of tourists wanting a photograph with him, the sausages were excellent, the breakfasts in the cafés delicious and the parks were full of cute she-dogs and she-humans.

As the three women chatted animatedly as they had done at the National Theatre, Etta's attention was drawn to a picture on a little table next to her.

"Isn't that Mr Janda?" she asked, pointing to the group of people in the shot.

"Exactly right. That photo was taken when I worked at the Embassy," Marketa explained.

Dora looked at the picture too.

"And that's Mr Zima, although he looks much younger there."

"We all looked younger in those days," sighed Marketa.

"Not at all, you're no different now," said Dora, pointing to a cheerful young Marketa. "You looked like a Hollywood actress. And this striking woman with big smile and prominent cheekbones… I feel I should know her, too."

"Don't you recognise her?" Marketa asked, picking the photo up from the table and showing it to both women. "I'm sure you know her, and she certainly has much more in common with Hollywood than I do."

Etta and Dora looked at the woman. The impression that they

should recognise her was overwhelming, but for the life of them, no name came to mind.

"She was the US Ambassador here during the Velvet Revolution years." Marketa tried to help them. "Maybe think of her blonder, her hair curlier, and definitely younger…"

The two women shook their heads. They didn't have a clue.

"*The Good Ship Lollipop*…" Marketa whispered.

"*Shirley Temple*?" Etta and Dora cried in unison, waking poor Leon from his dream of a walk in the Castle Gardens with the most charming of she-Bassets at his side.

"It *is* her, I recognise her features now," said Dora.

"The same smile." Etta nodded. "But what was she doing at the Embassy?"

"Shirley Temple Black, as she was known then, was the US Ambassador in Prague from 1989 to 1992," declared Marketa with such pride, it was as if the former actress had been her daughter.

"Really?" asked Etta, still bewildered.

"She was a great Ambassador at that."

"Was that after the Velvet Revolution, when things quietened down?"

"No, she was appointed by President Bush during the most critical time in the summer of 1989. She presented her credentials in August and actively helped our country turn into a democracy in the most peaceful way possible by the end of the year."

"And I thought she was just a cinema diva! How could she handle such a crucial political transition?"

"Most people knew her as Curly Top, but there was much more to her than that. After all, she'd only been a Hollywood star during her childhood. Later, she'd started working for the UN, then became an Ambassador in Africa…"

"You mean she was appointed for her expertise as a diplomat, not her fame as an actress?"

"That is beyond doubt. When the US Government sent her to

Prague during those precarious months, they knew good things would come from the appointment. Shirley Temple the curly-haired child had grown into a resolute woman, a pragmatic diplomat. And besides, she had a bone to pick with Prague."

"Really?"

"You know," said Marketa, leaning forward as if she were about to tell a long tale, her eyes glittering with the joy of sharing that empowers every storyteller, "I'm sure we determine the course of our life for the most part, but I would never deny that Fate plays a role, too, and at times, it's got a heavy hand. At other times, it's so gentle, you can barely perceive it. In the case of Shirley – I call her by her first name because she asked me to – Fate played a big role…"

"You mean it was her destiny to become Ambassador in Prague?" Dora leant forward too, not wanting to miss a single word.

"Oh no, I'm sure she made a conscious decision to take the role, and she was the best person who could have covered the position."

"So what's all the Fate nonsense about?" Etta asked.

"Fate entered Shirley's life in August 1968. By chance, she happened to be in Prague during our darkest days…"

"Working for the Embassy?"

"Not at all, she was in Prague to make a speech as a representative of the Multiple Sclerosis International Federation. It was at a time when we – the Czechoslovakians as we were then – believed there had to be a way to find peace, a natural way out of dictatorship. Under leaders such as Alexander Dubček, who proclaimed there could be 'Socialism with a human face', our country experienced the Prague Spring. We had many reforms: liberalisation, freedom of thought and speech, the arts flourished, and we opened up to Western organisations such as the one Shirley was in. Then after her speech at Charles University, the Czechs agreed to join the international federation."

59

"And did she meet Dubček? Even in Italy, the man was held in great admiration as an important reformer."

"No, they were scheduled to meet on the day of Shirley's speech, but he had to make sudden changes to his plans. Nonetheless, he said he'd be pleased to meet her the next day, but Shirley was due to leave for America. Her family was waiting for her as she'd been away for a week…"

"I still don't see where Fate comes into this story," grumbled Etta.

"Have a little patience," Marketa reprimanded her. "Don't you know what happened that night?"

"August 1968, you said?"

"That's right, but it wasn't the first or the second, or the tenth or eleventh. Nope, it was the twentieth of August."

Etta looked at the nurse without understanding, but Dora, who'd been reading her guides and books carefully, knew exactly what the woman was referring to.

"The night the Soviets invaded Prague."

8

A TALE FROM THE PAST

Marketa nodded, her face dark. It was as if, even after so many years, she could still feel the pain.

"Exactly," she said. "That evening, Shirley went back to her room in the Alcron Hotel, close to Wenceslas Square. The press conference had gone on for so long, she'd skipped her dinner. In her bag, she found some Droste pastilles her children had put in there and made do with them. Then she went to sleep, only to be awoken early the next morning by someone at her door, shouting that the Soviets had invaded the town, seized the airport and were now walking the streets, shooting people.

"Shirley went up onto the hotel roof, crouching low on the parapet. Due to the hotel's strategic position, she could see it all: endless columns of tanks rolling into every street, thousands of stern-faced soldiers marching along the cobbled alleys, weapons everywhere. Helpless, the Czech people wandered amongst them, too dumbfounded even to be afraid, maybe asking them what was happening, what were they doing there. The size of the invading army was simply overwhelming, but even worse was to come.

"From the direction of Wenceslas Square, she heard machine guns firing. Shirley went back inside the Alcron Hotel, trying to get information on what was happening, but it soon became clear that her way out of the country had been blocked. She was afraid for her family; the thought that she might never see her young children again crossed her mind. Nonetheless, she was a strong woman who would always see things through. She felt it was her duty to witness what was happening, what the Soviets were doing...

"When she heard the rumble of the tanks close to the hotel, she looked outside from the lobby. A woman, completely unarmed, was asking for mercy for herself and her family. A shot rang through the air, and before Shirley realised what was happening, the woman dropped dead in the middle of the street, a few metres away from her."

"Oh my goodness!" cried Dora, twisting her hands.

"Yes, the Soviets destroyed every hope we had. We Czechs were not meant to have an easy life, along with all the other countries that were invaded by the Nazis first, and then ended up under Communism. After World War II, we had such high hopes of freedom and a better life, but darkness took over once again. Then in 1968, it seemed we could almost touch freedom and democracy, but yet again, we were thwarted and pulled down into the abyss.

"But Shirley, she was no ordinary woman. She found herself driving the US Embassy van through unfamiliar streets, as the original driver had been called up by the police. She caught up with him a few kilometres ahead and helped him lead the convoy of a hundred vehicles, full of American citizens and those from other countries, as they made a bid for the safety of West Germany.

"Shirley and the driver took it in turns as they negotiated frightening checkpoints manned by Soviet or Czech soldiers. It took long hours before the convoy reached the West German border. But at the end of a very long day, they made it back into the free world."

"It's like a scene from one of her movies," said Dora, seeing it all in her mind's eye. "Driving a van, leading a convoy…"

"Exactly what she used to say: 'I could be brave because I had done such brave things in my movies that no extraordinary thing seemed too extraordinary, even in real life.'"

"And what happened then?" asked Etta.

"Once in Germany, she could fly back to the States. But she swore she'd never forget the woman who fell in front of her eyes. It was there and then that she realised what her mission in life was: she wanted to be more involved in bringing democracy to other countries.

"The day after her return, she started to study, reading all sorts of newspapers and books, and she told her husband, Charles Black, she wanted to play an active role on the international scene. That's when she began working with the United Nations, and later she was appointed Ambassador in Ghana. Then finally, she came back to Prague."

"I see what you mean now," said Dora, shocked and wanting to know more in equal measures. "It was Fate that ensured she was in Prague on the day the Soviets invaded, but it was not just pure chance that she became the US Ambassador in Prague in 1989. She'd wanted that badly and moulded her life so that she could be there again when she was needed."

Marketa squeezed Dora's arm in empathy. "That's exactly the case. In 1989, she closed a circle that had opened up 21 years earlier."

Etta, as usual, was more sceptical. "Are you saying that without her, you would not have become a democracy?"

"I'm sure the time was right for Czechoslovakia to become a democracy, but do you remember the bloodshed in Romania? Here, even as late as January 1989, we had police brutality repressing crowds of students, and every demonstration after that took place under the threat of drastic military reaction. I'm no historian; I can't categorically say that without Mrs Temple

Black, things would have gone differently, and of course, all other countries' diplomatic efforts played their part. But I know she fought hard, and the US President was smart in sending her over.

"You see, everybody still thought of her as Curly Top. It's a well-known story that when the Communist President Gustáv Husák and his wife met her, they told her what great fans they had been of her movies. Husák was well aware that as an American, she was an enemy of the Communist system, but at the same time, she was not the classic suit-and-tie Ambassador. As she used to say, 'Shirley Temple opened doors for Shirley Temple Black.'" The nurse chuckled lightly. "She wasn't above a bit of playacting, even then."

"Playacting?" asked Etta, more engrossed in the tale than she'd like to admit and not wanting to interrupt the flow with any more words.

"Yes, because Shirley was no longer Curly Top; she was a woman who'd experienced the world, had strong views on what was right and wrong. But Hollywood had taught her how the admiration that comes from fame could win people over, so she knew when to be tough and when to be sweet.

"Mind you, she was fair and clear about her views. At the same time, she knew you couldn't change things by pure stubbornness or self-righteousness, but by dialogue. She had such a special way of handling people, as if she could not wait to bring out the best in them. And that changed people's views more than you would ever think possible – no one wanted to be a disappointment in Mrs Temple Black's eyes.

"Of course, she had her fair share of enemies. I'm sure Vasíl Bílak, the hardliner of the Czech Communist Party, simply hated her, but she even knew how to handle him."

"So what happened?" asked Dora, enraptured by this side to Shirley Temple she had never considered before.

"From the very first moment she set foot in the Embassy, Shirley spent time getting to know her staff. She presented her credentials to President Husák and got in touch with the other

European Embassies, but she also wanted to meet with dissidents, people from Charter 77, those who were writing the clandestine magazines, and also Alexander Dubček, the reformer she hadn't managed to meet in 1968, along with the future President Václav Havel, a writer who dedicated his life to the pursuit of freedom for Czechoslovakia."

"What are the clandestine magazines?"

"They were not necessarily anti-Communist propaganda – not at face value, at least – but they showed Czechoslovaks what life was like in the rest of the world, something the Communist regime didn't approve of. And Shirley got to know people like Josef Janda and Egon Zima because they were not only local entrepreneurs, but also sympathisers with the dissidents. And that, of course, put them at risk, too; it wouldn't have been enough to tell the STB – the secret Czech police – you knew nothing about the dissidents. People were sent to jail and hard labour camps for much less than an accusation of being a sympathiser.

"But when Shirley got to know about this danger, she insisted on meeting them. It was important for her that members of society supported actions against the Government; she interpreted it as a sign that the people were becoming less afraid, that the harsh repression after the Prague Spring was wearing off, that the Czechoslovaks were ready to fight again for democracy."

"You've mentioned she met Zima and Janda frequently, but what about Ms Kladivova? Did Mrs Temple Black ever meet her?"

"Eva Kladivova was not as involved or as active as Zima and Janda, but she did allow some of her staff to make photocopies in her office. I went there myself a few times to deliver some of the material to be distributed. And yes, Shirley met her, too, but I wasn't present on those occasions. I know Eva admitted to being amongst those who'd signed the Charter 77 petition, albeit more recently than its founders.

"As for Shirley, she was meeting lots of people who had signed Charter 77, the document accusing the Government of not respecting human rights as laid out in the Helsinki Agreement. Like the clandestine magazines, Charter 77 was not expressly anti-Communism; that would be too dangerous and would, in the eyes of the authorities, justify a strong reaction.

"She made a good friend of Brother Benedikt, a man who'd seen first-hand the terrors of prisons, concentration camps and the uranium mines, where he had been forced to work for years as a young monk. But once he was back in Prague, despite health problems, he signed Charter 77. He wanted the freedom to profess his own thoughts and religion. I introduced the two of them, and I was so glad when they became friends.

"Now well aware of how things worked, Shirley wanted to be informed of any actions taken against the dissidents by the STB. Then she'd ask the authorities why each person had been detained and remind them how important it was if Czechoslovakia really wanted to get in the Most Favoured Nations list for trade agreements with the US – and President Husák was very keen on that idea – to show respect for all citizens' human rights, as set out in the Helsinki Agreement."

"Didn't her attitude provoke a strong reaction from the Communists?"

"It did, but while Ambassadors cannot question a country's inner politics, they can ask its leaders to comply with international treaties they have signed. Of course, there were quarrels and discussions, but she kept going, sometimes with a smile, sometimes with a stern word.

"She was a tirelessly hard worker. Every evening, no matter how long the working day had been, where she'd travelled, she'd sit down and write her cables to the United States. When, as a nurse, I recommended she take a little rest, take it easy, she'd reply, 'I can't. I saw that woman dying in front of me in 1968 and I'll do my very best to make sure no one else ends up a victim of a similar atrocity.' And she was very upfront with Washington:

she wasn't asking for advice; she'd tell US Government what to do. She'd ask them to welcome visiting Czech delegations, to be friendly, but not to concede anything to them until they'd promised to adhere to the Human Rights agreements."

"Did she get impatient when President Husák or the other ministers didn't listen?"

"Oh no. She used to say that her stay in Africa had taught her patience and to have a different sense of time. In Ghana, she had to switch her mentality from 'here and now' to 'it will take the time it takes, but we will get there'. However, she'd put her days to good use: if she wasn't meeting the locals, she'd be in touch with all the embassies and authorities around Europe; she wanted the Czechoslovak Government to feel they were under special surveillance. As long as they felt the whole world was looking at them, they might refrain from committing atrocities...

"After a few weeks in Prague, Shirley was convinced the time was right, that change would soon be sweeping the country. But she also feared, from what Havel, Dubček and Brother Benedikt had told her, that a brutal reaction could come from the Government out of fear of losing all they stood for, so she doubled down on her work. She asked to meet more members of the Government; she wanted to be constantly in touch with them to make sure they didn't resort to violence. I really feared she was overworking herself, but she seemed to thrive on the pressure. Now I see that she understood what was happening before we, the Czechoslovak citizens, did.

"During the Autumn of 1989, more unauthorised peaceful demonstrations took place. The hundreds of students in the streets became thousands of people, then tens of thousands, facing up to menacing armed cops wearing full riot gear. On 17 November 1989, there was a demonstration to remember the students massacred by the Nazis in 1939. The crowds swelled to over a hundred thousand participants, and by 20 November, half a million citizens of Prague were demonstrating peacefully on the streets of the city. An ocean of people, finally immune to fear, were chanting *'Kde domov můj'* – where my home is – our National Anthem.

"When Havel and Dubček made their famous speech in Wenceslas Square, people were crying out with joy. And Shirley had not missed a moment of these events, making sure the Czechoslovak Government and the foreign press knew she was there.

"Then the news came through: the entire Central Committee had resigned. There would be no military intervention, which meant this event would go down in history as the Velvet Revolution."

"That must have been such a joyous day."

"It was indeed," said Marketa proudly, wiping away a tear that had dared to run down her cheek. "Remember, this came about not after one or even a few years of darkness; it was after decades. It still saddens me that some Czechs were born under Nazism and died under Communism without ever seeing the light of freedom."

"Oh!" cried Dora. Of course, she had read all about Czech history in books, but it was so different to hear it from a person who had lived through it all.

Marketa smiled. She had explained the country's darkest hours; now she wanted to indulge in the happy ones.

"That day, back at the Embassy, Ambassador Temple Black summoned all of her closest staff into the conference room. We had been working hard for this moment and expected a celebratory speech. But surprisingly, after she had locked the doors, she looked straight into our faces, one after the other. Her features tightened, her voice was almost menacing as she spoke.

"'I'm only going to do this once,' she said, 'just once.' Then her face broke into a smile, her feet started to move, her voice sang as she tap-danced all around the room, and we laughed and clapped along to the rhythm."

While Leon continued to snore placidly on the floor, Dora

broke down in tears. Etta, trying in vain to hide her emotions, mumbled that she had choked on a biscuit crumb.

Marketa held the photograph to her heart for a few seconds.

"So that was Mrs Shirley Temple Black, inexhaustible and forever an optimist. Rather than waiting for the good things to happen, she did all that was needed to turn her – and our – dreams into reality. I will never forget her."

9

THE STRAHOV MONASTERY

Marketa took them on a tour, walking along a tiny road, cobbled as most streets seemed to be in Prague and flanked by tall walls, behind which the branches of trees and vegetation were emerging. The road was so narrow that Etta wondered what they'd do if a car tried to pass. Sensing danger behind, she turned back, only to find a group of tourists busy consulting a map. Or was the menacing presence beyond them, hiding in an alcove along the wall?

Maybe it was just her overexcited imagination. When she and Dora had visited Prague Castle and St Vitus Cathedral the day before, she had had the uneasy feeling of being not only observed, but followed. Without doubt, murders had an adverse effect on her mood.

The end of the road took them into a large square. A huge Baroque palace was on their right, stretching the entire length of the square. The Černín Palace, Marketa explained, was the seat of the Foreign Ministry, but Dora was more interested in the beautiful white façade opposite the palace. This building's windows and cornerstones were painted in a mustard yellow that shined as if made of gold. Add in a charming onion-shaped bell tower, a few spires and a balustrade decorated with evocative statues, many of angels for which she had a real passion, and she was clasping her hands at the beauty of it all.

This was the Loreta Monastery, Marketa continued, where the Holy House of the Virgin Mary was guarded, a replica of the original one that, according to folklore, the angels had carried from Nazareth to Loreto in Italy in 1294 when the Holy Land fell into the hands of the Turks.

"I saw the original with our Parish priest, Don Peppino," said Dora. "He organises trips all over Italy and Europe."

Etta sighed. She too remembered the trip to Recanati and Loreto, but she hadn't particularly enjoyed it. The coach from Castelmezzano had been filled with the village's most elderly inhabitants and she had come face to face with old age, something she dreaded deeply. They'd had to stop every hour or so as the travellers needed the toilet, including once in the middle of the countryside, and there had been so much talk of the Second World War, it was as if it had only happened last week.

"You can come here any time you like for a visit, but today, I thought I'd take you to the Strahov Monastery. I had to book your tickets in advance, but as you'll see, it's a real jewel."

"Will they allow Napoleon in?" asked Dora. The Basset had been happy about their visit to the castle the previous day, for he had been allowed to play in the grounds while she and Etta had taken it in turns to visit the interior.

"I'm afraid not, which is such a shame. Most of the visit is indoors and Leon won't be allowed in." The hound's ears plunged to the ground. "But the monastery is set in a huge park and I'd be delighted to show him around for you. I'm sure we'll meet some other dogs, too."

This sounded better. Leon's ears rose again while Dora looked at Marketa in gratitude.

The Monastery was crowded, but fortunately, the guided tour was for a small group of people. While an Englishman who thought he knew it all monopolised the guide's attention with the most impossible and pointless questions, despite his wife's frantic attempts to shut him up, Dora gazed around her in delight. Of all the strange things in the Cabinet of Curiosities, she particularly loved the xylotheque – the 'ancient books' that were, in fact, cases made out of wood. The title on the spine of each was actually the type of tree the wood came from, and inside the cases were pieces of bark, roots, branches and, where relevant, dried fruits and blossoms.

"Wouldn't it be lovely to have the same at home for all our favourite trees?" she asked Etta.

"Your collection of *Pippi Longstocking* volumes from every country we visit, and the collection of angels, and the Christmas tree decorations, and all sorts of artworks from your students… I think we've got more than enough. Any more and we'll have to start charging people an admission fee when they visit our house."

The guide was announcing that the moment had come to enter the Theological Hall when the Englishman interrupted her again.

"The Theological Hall was designed in the XVII century by Italian architect Giovanni Domenico Orsi. You will recognise the typical stucco works on the ceilings, very much the Baroque style. A bit too ostentatious for my taste, although I must say, the austerity of the bookcases below counteract the Italian extravaganza…"

"I can't understand," said Etta, looking at him with uncharacteristically admiring eyes, "why you spent time and money on a flight and hotel."

The man had puffed himself up, readying himself for a compliment, but he was taken aback by her question and gazed at her with a quizzical expression.

"It's evident," continued Etta, her tone of her voice changing abruptly from sugary sweet to derogatory, "you have seen it all on Google. I'm sure the guide will give you a prize at the end of the tour, and I will gladly contribute to that if you would just keep your mouth SHUT until then."

"I told you so," his wife cried in embarrassment while the guide looked at Etta with a smile of gratitude and two other couples on the tour mimed clapping their hands. Then, the guide finished her explanation without interruption and let them in.

The beautiful Theological Library – despite what the Englishman had said – demanded respect, with its oak floors and ancient globes. The cases against the walls displayed over twenty thousand books, while the décor on the barrel-vaulted ceiling alternated between fresco paintings and rich stucco. Completely different was the larger and taller Philosophical Hall with its walnut interiors and *The Intellectual Progress of Mankind* fresco, God in the centre of the great Greek philosophers.

"You're not there yet, what a shame!" said Etta to the Englishman as she scrutinised the painting as if looking for his portrait. The others on the tour, the man's wife and the guide included, guffawed as his face went Titian red with ill-concealed rage.

Once they exited the monastery into the fresh air outside, it took a while for Etta's mind to clear from the treasures they had just seen. They were spotted by Leon and Marketa, the hound barely wiggling his tail a couple of times at them. It was clear he wanted to go back to the park where he'd spent a happy time with Marketa.

"Leon met a lovely female Basset Hound by the name of Guendaline," Marketa explained. "It was difficult to remind him we had to catch up with you two."

Leon sighed heavily. Yes, he had just met the sweetest of she-Bassets – the one he had seen at the window opposite his new home. And up close, she was even more lovely, and charming, and delicate, and…

"The owner said they often visit Petřín park, and as you live off Malostranské náměstí, it's closer than it would be from my house. If you want, I can show you the way."

Etta looked at her watch. "It's almost six o'clock. I suggest we accompany you home – after all, you've already spent most of your day with us."

"It's been a real pleasure. While waiting for you, I enquired about Brother Benedikt, the friend I introduced to Shirley Temple Black, but he no longer lives at Strahov. He's at Břevnov now."

"Břevnov?" asked Dora.

"Yes, it's another monastery a good walk from Strahov in the western part of town. It's well worth a visit, especially if you want to try one of the best beers in Prague…"

"I thought you said it was a monastery, not a bar," said Dora.

"It is. Monks have a history of taking care of body *and* spirit. They brew a beer that alone is worth the visit, and the place is gorgeous, too. We have more than our fair share of castles and monasteries in Prague – I'm amazed they survived the Communists."

10

DANGER CREEPS IN THE SHADOWS

Despite Leon's reluctance to leave the monastery grounds, they not only accompanied Marketa back home, but sat at her table for what the host called a 'quick-fix dinner', which the guests found to be both abundant and tasty. Etta and Dora found out the special secret of Prague's beer, too: it went down so smoothly, they forgot they were not in actual fact drinking cappuccinos.

When they finally left the cosy interior of Marketa's house, it was dark.

"Do you think we're drunk?" asked Dora, unused to drinking any more than a glass of wine when they had guests back home.

"No, we're simply getting to know the local customs."

"Maybe we shouldn't indulge in those customs too much more. I dread to think what will become of us when we visit Scotland with all those whisky distilleries..."

If it weren't for Leon guiding them along the lane they had walked in the sunlight of the morning, the two women probably wouldn't have found their way. Despite their woozy state, though, Etta still felt a presence behind her. She turned back but, with her head spinning as if she were on a Tagada ride, it took her a while to focus on what she was seeing. To be fair, the darkness didn't help.

When she finally realised that if she concentrated on a fixed point, her eyes would stop dancing, she decided she must be more drunk than she'd thought. She saw not just one shadow hiding in an alcove, but a second one 20 metres or so behind.

"Am I seeing double or hallucinating?" But the dog was serene and she had learned to trust Leon's instinct. He only seemed interested in the road and its smells. And he was the one who had not been drinking beer.

Coming out of the narrow Černínská Street, they found themselves facing the Loreta Monastery. In the darkness, made even more mysterious by the dim yellow streetlights, the procession of statues looked murky and intimidating, their shadows creeping over the pavements as if they would leave their pedestals any minute and prowl among the living.

The sound of footsteps came from behind them, and this time both women turned, but the sound died away the second they did so and the square was empty.

Adrenaline cleared the fog enveloping Etta's thoughts, her brain getting back to work.

"I believe Leon is taking the road to the park. I'd say we'd be better off cutting through the Castle square. I'm sure we will find other people there." Yes, the very people she wanted to avoid during the day now offered the reassurance she craved. They turned to the left, but Leon was determined to take his long detour for two reasons: one, curious Bassets *always* prefer the longer road, unless it's dinner time or raining; two, sweetest Guendaline was used to taking night walks, and if he could catch a little of her scent here and there, wouldn't that console his lonely heart? But his two humans were deaf to his pleas. He was brutally dragged their way, wondering whether he had a case for putting his Basset superpowers to use. This hound could not only glue his bum to the asphalt, he could multiply his weight a hundred times.

He sat. As Etta pulled at his leash angrily, she saw it beyond any doubt. A shadow detached itself from the darkness of its hiding place and sprinted towards them.

Does he mean to harm us? Dora's eyes seemed to ask. She'd seen it too.

What else? Etta's glare telegraphed.

Desperately, they pulled together at the leash, but the dog remained completely unaware of the threat.

"Please, Leon! Can't you see Prague's answer to Jack the Ripper is almost upon us?" cried Etta frantically. "You'll be served up for someone's breakfast in the morning."

But just like the worst of nightmares, the monster was hurtling towards them and they were standing still, unable to move.

The footsteps clanged along the middle of the paved road. It was a man, without doubt, and he was running straight at them. There was not a car nor another soul in sight.

Etta and Dora screamed. Leon did not budge an inch. When the impact seemed unavoidable, Etta could only close her eyes and have a word with the powerful Creator of all things small and large, useful and useless, alive and dead.

"I know I've criticised the way You do things at times, but it was not that I was being arrogant; I was just afraid no one was providing You with sincere feedback. I still think mosquitoes are totally useless, as are the large majority of men. I might be wrong, and maybe I'm seeing the world from one tiny corner. Maybe You had something great in mind for men and mosquitoes, but You might want to have a look at them every now and then, make sure things haven't slipped out of hand and You really intended them to be the way they are.

"As for my daughter, Maddalena – I know how busy You are up there, but if You could, send a look her way every once in a while and make sure she's not doing anything stupid. I mean, she's got a degree in statistics, so why would she be tattooing people for a living?

"Now, I've been talking to You for quite a while. Maybe I'm already dead. Will I open my eyes and look down on my body torn to pieces? Will the dog be an array of meatballs? And mostly, why are the footsteps both multiplying and fading away? Is it my soul going up to heaven that's making things sound distant? That's good news – I have always been afraid You might misunderstand me and erroneously send me to hell..."

Etta summoned up all her courage and opened her right eye a tiny bit, ready to shut it again rapidly if the view was of blood and splattered intestines. The Basset was still sitting stubbornly in the same place; Dora was all in one piece and looking at something going on ahead of them. Etta opened both eyes to follow Dora's gaze and distinguished two figures running. Then one grabbed the other's collar and dragged him towards the women.

"Sorry if I scared you," said a male voice whilst gurgles and muffled protests came from the other man, "but do you know this guy?"

By the light of a cast-iron lamp, Etta and Dora recognised the wry smile of Mr Smolak, holding the other man with his arm folded behind his back, his face towards the two women. Etta thought of the hollow cheeks and deep brown eyes of the man she'd seen at the café in Nový Svět, but no, this was a sturdy young man with a square face and very short hair. He was in no way familiar to either woman, so they shook their heads.

"Why were you following them?" Smolak asked his captive.

"I wasn't," the other protested, grinding his teeth.

"Hasn't your mum taught you not to tell lies?" Mr Smolak must have been twisting his captive's arm a bit because the young man gave a cry. "I've been on your heels since I arrived in Nový Svět just in time to see you following these two women..."

"I wasn't!" The captive grimaced in pain. Then he kicked his foot against Mr Smolak's legs. As the older man stumbled, the other pushed him to the ground and ran away as fast as he could.

"Mr Smolak, are you OK?" Dora cried, looking at him sprawled on the ground.

"I was much better a couple of seconds ago, although I didn't know it at the time." The two women helped him get up as the man grumbled about how stupid he had been to let his captive escape so easily.

"Oh no! Think how lucky it was that you should be here," said Dora, looking at him with grateful eyes.

"That was indeed good luck," the man said, nodding seriously. "The closing dinner to mark the end of the conference was held for all the guests near the castle, and afterwards, I decided to take a walk before heading back to my hotel. Nový Svět and Loretánská have always been among my favourite parts of Prague. Then I noticed that man hiding behind a row of cars. When you came out of one of the doors – I recognised Leon and knew it was you – he started following you. I was making sure not to alert him to my presence, but when I saw him running as if to assault you... well, you know what happened next."

"I wonder what he wanted from us," said Etta pensively.

"Are you sure you've never seen him before?"

The two women shook their heads. They were positive they hadn't.

"And what about you?" Etta added. "Have you seen him before? I take it he wasn't at the concert, nor at the conference."

"I will have a look at all the photos from both events, but I doubt it. I'm rather good at remembering people's faces. So, are you heading home? You mentioned Malostranské náměstí the other day..."

"Yes, that's where we're staying," said Dora. The man led them towards the Castle square, Leon now following without too much fuss, although he wasn't particularly disturbed by what had happened. His mind was on Guendaline alone.

"Why do you think a man we've never met would be following us?" asked Etta.

"Either he has something to do with the murder or you have already made some enemies in Prague…"

"Of course we haven't!" cried Etta, horrified that someone could think they were anything other than two lovable ladies.

"But then again, even if he has something to do with the murder, why would he be following you?"

"That I can't understand, in all honesty," said Etta. "Unless…"

"Unless?"

"Well, they say that the murderer returns to the crime scene. If he had been on Charles Bridge early Saturday morning, he'd have seen us speaking to the police…"

"I see," said Mr Smolak. "And then he may have followed you, seen you pick up the lipstick compact on the Legion Bridge, speak to Janda, and finally return to talk to the police again with a piece of evidence in your hands."

"And he might have seen us speaking to you – someone from the Embassy who knew most of the people there…"

"Do you think when he saw us speaking to Marketa, he might have felt threatened?" asked Dora.

"I'm not sure," said the man, thinking out loud. "Marketa no longer works at the Embassy, but she was present the night of the murder. Did she tell you if she noticed anything unusual that night?"

"Not at all," said Dora.

"I'm not even sure she knew Ms Kladivova," Smolak said pensively.

"She did – she told us about Eva Kladivova's past, how she was involved in helping the dissidents before the Velvet Revolution, although she did not visit the Embassy as regularly as other people like Janda and Zima."

"I see," the man said. "Anything else that might be related to Friday night's murder?"

"No, I'm afraid we mainly spoke about the past. She told us

about Mrs Shirley Temple Black; we didn't even know she was an Ambassador."

The man smiled, but it was an automatic smile. Maybe he wanted to concentrate on the present.

"Did you know her?" Dora asked.

"Who?"

"Mrs Temple Black."

"Of course. I started to work at the Embassy at the time she was appointed Ambassador. She was a talented woman, but I was thinking of this murder. I fear that young man I so foolishly allowed to escape might be working for our killer. Maybe he's an assassin, hired to kill Ms Kladivova. I think you'd better stop your sleuthing right now and speak to the police as early as possible in the morning."

They had reached Malostranské náměstí and the dog led them all to the front of their building on one of the side streets. The main door was closed and locked, and they needed a second key to access a wrought-iron gate inside. And the CCTV cameras were on. Mr Smolak seemed to be satisfied by the security system, but nonetheless, he reminded them to speak to the police the next morning.

11

SIMPLE TOURISTS

The next morning, Etta and Dora did as Mr Smolak had suggested and called Lieutenant Baloun. The policeman seemed neither surprised nor worried about their frightening experience the previous night.

"I'm busy in Holešovice today – there's another spate of cocaine dealing. Apparently, the rich can't do without the stuff or they will lose all their money-making skills. But I'll tell you what, if you've been snooping – and I hope you haven't – you must stop this ridiculous exercise. A thief can be a dangerous person to cross. But I'm sure after Mr Smolak dealt with him, the guy who was after you last night will avoid you for a while. That is as long as you stay away from trouble."

"A thief?" Etta cried. "You don't believe the murder was a robbery gone wrong after all we've discovered, do you?"

"I don't have any reason to think otherwise."

"But that's just silly! How can you not take into account the concert and its guests, Ms Eva Kladivova's strange expression when she looked at Mr Janda, and now this attack on us. I think he's been following us for days – why would he do that if he was just a simple thief after our handbags?"

"I don't think the man following you was the killer, if that's what you're hinting at."

"Maybe a hitman," pressed Etta.

"Maybe," the Lieutenant said, unconvinced. "I will come to see you tomorrow morning, first thing. For today, just be tourists. Prague is such a wonderful city – why don't you go and visit the Town Hall or Vyšehrad or the Jewish quarter? There's so much to see, just forget about the case."

"That's exactly what we were doing yesterday, until someone decided to follow us…"

"As I said, I feel confident they will no longer represent a problem for you, as long as you mind your own business. I need to go now. Don't do anything silly."

The man put down the phone, leaving Etta and Dora flabbergasted.

"How can he be so sure we're no longer in danger?" said Etta. Leon, however, was of the same mind as the Lieutenant. He was pointing towards the door, ready to go out for a long walk in the not-so-secret hope of meeting Guendaline.

"Let's go to see some of the places Marketa mentioned yesterday, I need some fresh air to clear my thoughts," grumbled Etta. "I find it rather disturbing the way the Lieutenant simply dismissed us; I was expecting more concern over what might have happened to us."

"Maybe he's simply too busy…"

"Everyone's told us the crime rate is low in Prague. Even drugs for the rich and wealthy can't be – shouldn't be – more important than people's lives. Shall we tell Christine?"

"She'll be busy today working on the roadshow that follows the conference. And she will tell our hosts, who will have their holidays ruined by their concern for us…"

"But we need to compare notes with a local. Maybe Christine will understand the police's attitude, as frankly, I can't."

"We could phone Marketa instead, thank her again for dinner

and invite her to our place tomorrow. Then we can ask her what she thinks."

With a grunt of acquiescence, Etta agreed. But the nurse's mobile went straight to voicemail. A voice, first in Czech and then in English, informed them the phone was switched off and invited them to leave a message. Etta phoned Marketa at home, but had no more luck: the phone rang, but no one picked up the call.

"Oh, well. Shall we just go out and do as the Lieutenant suggested?" wondered Etta.

For once, it was ever naïve, never suspicious Dora who erred on the side of caution. "What if we write a letter to Christine first?"

"Why?"

"So that if something happens to us," Dora explained, "she will know what has been going on since Friday and what our thinking is."

"I really hope nothing will happen to us, but that might be a good idea."

"Should we use the 'envelope in the envelope' method and write something like 'Open only if something happens to us' on the inner one?"

"Sounds a bit dramatic, but it might work," Etta conceded.

"Still, she will be worried when she receives it."

"How about leaving it with the lady on the ground floor? We could tell her that if she doesn't see us for a day or so, then she should post the letter."

"That sounds like a good idea. She isn't likely to be alarmed as Christine might be, but she will notice if we don't return one evening."

"And if everything turns out fine, we can just ask her to return the letter to us."

To the poor, patient Basset, this latest development was a terrible blow. As the two women returned the leash to the coat rack and sat down at the table, he launched into his trademark trio of loud WOOFs in protest, but the harridans simply didn't care. The world could be so cruel to an innocent soul such as he. He returned hopefully to the window, but alas, the flat opposite was all shut up, the lovely she-Basset probably in the park wondering what her favourite he-hound was up to. With a heavy heart, Leon went to find solace under the large piano.

As Dora wrote on a piece of paper, Etta elaborated on what she had already noted down. They detailed the mysterious man's attack and Mr Smolak's rescue, describing the indifference of the police official and recounting their sleuthing on the day the murder victim was found.

"In case something should happen to us," the letter ended, "please show this document to the police, possibly to an officer of higher rank than Lieutenant Baloun, who seems less concerned with the danger following us than he ought to be."

"What if we're wrong about that and ruin his career?" asked Dora, feeling they may have been a little too harsh.

"If we're wrong," said Etta drily, "nothing will happen to us, so no one will ever read this letter."

"No, I mean what if something bad does happen, but the Lieutenant wasn't being intentionally mean to us?"

"Miss Dorotea Rosa Pepe, there can be no grey area: either he was wrong about us not being in danger, or he was right."

Dora did not look totally convinced. Life could be complicated at times; it was not just a black and white thing. But it would be even more complicated to explain that to Etta.

Etta read the whole letter aloud again. Dora approved, despite her doubts. Leon yawned, and finally they set off, stopping on the ground floor to drop the letter off.

"I... I don't understand," stuttered their downstairs neighbour, a woman with wild blonde hair and bulging hazel eyes that seemed to be forever surprised at the strangeness of the world. "Why don't you send it directly to Mrs Coleman?"

"Because she might not even need to read this message," Etta explained patiently.

"Then why are you leaving it with me?"

"Just in case we go out and don't return."

"But why would you leave so soon when you've planned to stay for three weeks?"

"Because..."

"Because life happens!" Dora interrupted. "I'm sure you've planned things one way, but as it turns out, due to unforeseen circumstances, the opposite takes place."

"Oh yes," said the woman, understanding dawning in her expression. "That happens a lot. Actually, I'd say it's rare for things to go the way you planned."

"And that is why," continued Dora as assertively as she was able, "we'd like to make sure that, should life get in the way, should we suddenly disappear..."

The woman looked at her strangely.

"...not that we plan to disappear any time soon," Dora reassured her, "but should we have to leave sooner rather than later, we'll know there's a person who can explain things to Christine."

"But how can I explain if I know nothing?"

"You won't have to explain! Just hand her the letter and that will make it all clear."

"Now I see," she said, then grinned. "How clever!"

Etta was horrified that someone could be so slow; Leon had fallen asleep out of sheer desperation. At this rate, they'd waste the whole day.

～

HOURS, DAYS, MAYBE MONTHS LATER – IN HIS DESPAIR, LEON HAD lost all perception of time – the two harridans finally took leave of their neighbour and opened the large door to the street. A few steps and they were in Malostranské náměstí, the green-blue domes and spires of St Nicholas's Church silhouetted against the sky. But Leon's attempts to go to either Petřín or Kampa park were in vain. The bipeds dragged him on to the Old Town, where the crowds of tourists didn't have so much as a Yorkshire Terrier between them. The women stood and marvelled at the Old Town square, waiting an awfully long time for a blue clock to strike the hour, and yelling in delight when it did so and a carillon played music and strange figures came out of the wall. They called it an astronomical clock, but Leon was unimpressed. It didn't feature a Basset, nor any other noteworthy dog.

The women took it in turns to visit the Town Hall as hounds were not allowed in, but he was allowed to join the guided tour of the subterranean areas. Murky, mysterious and smelly, it was a tour Leon enjoyed quite a bit, but the softer human seemed rather uneasy. She said she couldn't believe families spent hours down here during the wartime bombing raids. The harsher human then asked if these vaults were used as nuclear bunkers, too, but the guide replied that no, it was only a Second World War shelter. The nuclear bunkers were created during the Cold War. They contained enough food to serve whole communities for two to three days, which sounded like a very sensible arrangement to Leon. Better to have as many provisions as possible in case of an emergency.

"Are there many nuclear bunkers?" Etta asked.

"They're scattered all over the city. Some people had their own shelters in their gardens. Now, they use them as garden sheds."

Leon wondered if he might find one of these bunkers full of food while digging in Kampa park. That is, if the two harridans ever allowed him to visit that dog's idea of heaven again.

～

THE TWO WOMEN HAD PACKED SANDWICHES, WHICH THEY ATE WHILE sitting in Wenceslas Square and letting 'the sight sink in'. Dora read aloud from her guidebook, explaining things that had happened there during the Velvet Revolution. Overall, though, it was rather an uneventful morning, and the afternoon, it seemed, would be no different. They walked through strange passages where they found a sculpture of a man riding a horse upside down, the animal's four legs hanging from the ceiling. Dora explained it was the work of Czech artist, David Černý, possibly a mocking reference to the equestrian statue of King Wenceslas in his eponymous square. Leon wondered, if the artist had really intended to mock the king, why he had not suspended him by the arms and legs with the horse riding on his back.

But the hound could not criticise the use of animals in human art for too long as lots of tourists asked to have a photo taken with him. He accepted because he was a generous dog, but his heart was on the other side of the Vltava River. Only when the two women promised him a walk in the Kampa island park did the poor doggie concede that life might be worth living, after all.

～

On the island, Dora and Etta spotted a little café on the riverside, its windows decorated with aromatic plants in cast-iron pots, and nice little tables laid out on the grass. It was the time of day when they were ready for a good slice of cake, and the café counter displayed a formidable selection.

Etta went for a carrot cake – not necessarily a Prague speciality, but it was her favourite. Dora preferred the *palačinky* – pancakes filled with berries and jam, and served with whipped cream and fresh fruit. Now these really were a Czech speciality. As for Leon, he refused to eat from the bowl a kind waiter offered to him.

"What's happened to the dog? Has he picked up a bug of some sort during our walk? Not a bad stomach, Leon, please. I'm not too keen on going out in the middle of the night after what happened yesterday…"

Little did she know! It was the heart, not the stomach that ailed him. Oh, Guendaline!

After the cakes had been devoured and the last glug of cappuccino had disappeared, Etta tried once more to contact Marketa. It was only then that she noticed a message from that very woman.

"Dear Dora and Etta, I'm so sorry, but I have to leave unexpectedly for the country as my cousin is not feeling well. I'll get in touch with you if I return to Prague before you leave. Thanks for your company, I really appreciated the time we spent together."

"That's rather sudden," said Dora. "Isn't it?"

"I guess falling sick does tend to be sudden…"

"True, but we've phoned her time and time again, and her mobile has never been connected. If someone in her family is sick, I'd expect her to keep it on at all times, so people can stay in touch."

"Maybe she was on a train. Connection can be an issue when you're travelling."

"Maybe," said Dora meditatively. "Why don't we phone her now to make sure she's arrived safely and to enquire after her cousin's health?"

"I'm not sure. She says she'll get in touch when she's back in Prague, so it sounds as if she doesn't want to be disturbed."

"But often people cut themselves off at the very moment they need help more than ever…"

"I can't understand what you're up to, Miss Pepe, but here's my phone and this is her number."

Dora pressed the call button. Again, she was taken straight to an automatic message telling her the number she was trying was unobtainable.

"It's as I suspected. Maybe they don't have good connection in the country," Etta suggested.

"You're right. I'm sure she will call us back."

But by the time the two women went to bed that night, no call had come through, and the phone remained silent in response to Etta's messages.

12

THE NURSE IS GONE

The next day, before they left home, Dora asked Etta to send one more message to the nurse asking her to get in touch. But the only message they received back was from Lieutenant Baloun, announcing he had a new emergency to attend to and would come to see them the next day instead. Thus free from any engagement, the trio spent their morning discovering the luscious Letna park. There were plenty of dogs: stylish poodles, an aristocratic she-greyhound, but to Leon's dismay, none had the charms of Guendaline.

At lunchtime, they ate their homemade sandwiches, sitting in the open air by the 23 metre tall metronome in the upper part of the park with a splendid view over the sinuous Vltava, its bridges and the city. Fresh and restored, they visited Villa Bílek, the house and laboratory of Prague sculptor František Bílek, located at the edges of the park and built, according to the artist's specifications, between 1910 and 1911.

Dora enjoyed both the Art Nouveau villa, designed to resemble a corn field, its columns being the sheaves of wheat, and Bílek's poignant sculptures. Leon was simply impatient to go back home, whilst Etta was grateful. For once, art had spoken to her and she too had enjoyed the visit rather than spending the whole time wondering what people saw in a so-called masterpiece that to her was either trivial or plainly disgraceful.

Then, a sudden realisation struck Dora. Instead of standing breathless in awe, gasping as she tried to imprint the villa's image in her memory, she actually articulated a few words.

"Goodness, it's late afternoon and we've still not heard from Marketa. Should we call at her house on the way home? Maybe her neighbours can tell us more..."

"If you really want to," Etta said grumpily. They had done so much walking, her feet were aching and begging for a long bath and a rest. "Although I can't see why. She's told us she's gone away, and why, and it sounded as if she didn't want to be disturbed."

But if there was one thing that Etta had learned in the past year, it was that sweet, amenable Dora could become as stubborn as the most stubborn of mules on certain – in truth, rare – occasions. Then, no one would convince her to deviate from her plan, and something told Etta she was facing one of those rare occasions right now.

So, back they went to the picturesque cobbles of Nový Svět. In the same café they'd called in to ask for directions on Monday, they enquired about Marketa, pretending to be unaware that she had left the city temporarily. But neither the waitress nor the owner, the blonde woman with the bright pink lipstick, knew anything.

"Are you sure she's not in her house? Try ringing her – she's always back home by this time."

The two women headed over to the ochre building that housed the nurse just in time to see her neighbour going into next door.

"Good evening, madam," Dora stopped her. The woman turned to look at them with an uncertain expression. "Do you speak any English?" Dora asked. The woman shook her head. "German?"

"A little," the other replied, seeming none too pleased to be using that language, either. But at least it was common ground.

"We are friends of Marketa Ciprova and we're looking for her, but it seems she's not at home and she's not answering her phone."

"Yes, she sent me a message saying she was going to visit her cousin. I heard some sounds coming from her house last night, so I figure she left then. It was an emergency…"

"I tried to call her earlier today, but got no answer. All we received was one message similar to the one you got."

"Well, that's that, then," said the woman, edging through the doorway with wide eyes as if something had scared her.

"Wait, do you think it's the cousin in Karlštejn she's gone to see?" Etta turned in the direction the woman was staring. A man with hollow cheeks and deep brown eyes was glaring back at her, and she recognised him as the same person she'd seen in the café the first time they had visited Nový Svět. There was no doubt in her mind now – he was looking right at them, his expression hard. Etta turned away and ignored him, paying attention to what Marketa's neighbour was saying.

"It has to be, because she's never mentioned having family elsewhere."

But there was something she was leaving unspoken. The demeanour of the woman – fear or doubt, or maybe both – told Etta she was not going to articulate it, whatever it was.

"Did you notice anything strange yesterday?" Etta asked instead.

"No, not really," said the woman, her wandering eyes saying the opposite.

"Can I leave our phone number with you? Please call us should Marketa get in touch with you."

The woman agreed and they exchanged numbers, then she closed the door on them. Etta imagined her expression morphing from apprehension to relief now that she'd got rid of them. As for the strange old man, he had disappeared, probably through the gate that led into the garden almost opposite. Etta tried to peer in, but it wasn't a public park, just the entrance to a private garden. Even so, it was rather large and seemed a little out of place here in the middle of a cobbled residential street. Then, she waved away all distractions to concentrate on the present.

"You know what, Miss Pepe?"

"What, Mrs Passolina?"

"I'm starting to believe you might be right. There's something weird about Marketa disappearing like this. That neighbour is clearly scared and there's something she didn't want to tell us, but she knows more, I'm sure of it."

"Should we inform the police?"

"After the Lieutenant's reaction yesterday morning? I doubt he will do anything at all, other than saying the woman has simply gone to visit her cousin."

"What should we do, then?"

"I think it's time to disturb our friend Christine. I can't think of anyone else who'd be willing to help."

~

CHRISTINE WAS RUSHED OFF HER FEET. SHE HAD FINISHED WITH THE conference only to have to get started with the roadshow, travelling across the Czech Republic, Slovakia and Hungary. But as soon as she was free in the evening, she phoned them back. No, she had no idea of what might have happened to Marketa. Why were they so sure she was not visiting her cousin's village as she'd said? No, Christine did not know the cousin's name, but once she was back in Prague, she could ask around. Was there anything else she could do for them?

"Maybe. Do you know what will happen to Ms Eva Kladivova's company?"

"That's a good question, but again, I'm afraid, I don't have an answer. It all depends on who stands to inherit, but I haven't heard anything…"

"Maybe you could ask around about that too?"

"I can certainly try. A few Prague-based entrepreneurs have come along for the roadshow and it will be quite natural to bring up the subject of poor Eva's untimely death..."

The line went quiet

"Are you still there?" asked Etta when Christine didn't speak for a few moments.

"Sorry, I was thinking. If you need first-hand information, you could speak to Vlastimila Vodova, Ms Kladivova's secretary. She's been with her since forever, so I'm sure she'll know more than anyone else. I can ask her to come to the Embassy as soon as I'm free... it won't be any time this week as we're heading for Bratislava, and then Budapest for the weekend, but I could ask her to join us at the Embassy next Monday."

To Etta, Monday sounded an awfully long time away.

"Can't we visit her straight away? Will the company be open?"

"I see, you're in a hurry. I believe the company will be closed to the public, but I wouldn't be surprised if Vlastimila were in to sort things out. I can ring her if you want and make an appointment for you."

"That'd be great."

A few minutes later, Christine rang back.

"Vlastimila will be waiting for you tomorrow at midday. The company office is in Karlin, Prague 8 – I'll give you the address and directions on how to get there via SMS so as to avoid any misunderstanding with the spelling. I told her you met Eva during the concert and were impressed by her personality, and then you had to identify her body for the police so you feel drawn to find out more about her..."

"That's exactly what this is all about."

"Really?"

"Sure."

"That's strange, because Mr Smolak told me you have an interest in sleuthing."

"That man is so very cheeky."

"I guess so. Anyway, while you're on the line, why don't we arrange a visit for you at the Embassy? If you could forward me details of your identification cards, I will make sure they issue permission for you. Does Monday suit you?"

"That'd be lovely. At what time?"

"If you come along at midday, I'll show you around the palace and gardens and the Gloriette, and then we could go out for lunch around 1pm."

"We'll be there."

"In the meantime, if you need anything else, Mr Smolak will be back in Prague tomorrow afternoon to meet with the Ambassador and a delegation from Bulgaria."

"That's kind of you," Etta said, thinking this information could turn out to be quite handy.

13

EVA KLADIVOVA'S SECRETARY

E arly the next morning, Lieutenant Baloun came by for a short visit, but only succeeded in making Etta more flustered than ever. The attack, he maintained, had to have been instigated by a drug addict who intended to rob them, but after Mr Smolak's intervention, he would never dare trouble them again. As for the nurse, of course she had gone to visit her cousin in the country, just as her message had said.

"Why doesn't she pick up the phone, then?" Etta asked, exasperated.

"Because nowadays, we all know who's calling on our mobile and we're free to choose whether to answer or not."

"You'll never catch Eva Kladivova's killer if all you do is dismiss any hypotheses put forward while your brain cells take a lifelong holiday."

By the time he left, Etta was simply happy to be heading out. While injustice grated on her, she knew she sometimes needed to take it easy. And despite the Lieutenant's lack of cooperation, they had an appointment later that day that should bring them closer to the truth.

～

AFTER A PLEASANT RIDE ON THE TRAM, THEY STOPPED RIGHT IN front of a modern building, its glass façade gleaming. As they entered, a middle-aged woman at reception looked at them with disdain, wrinkling her nose at both their appearance and the dog. In superior tones, she told them this was not the Tourist Information Office and looked even more dubious when they mentioned they had an appointment with Ms Vodova.

"I'll just check with her." Then she picked up the phone and launched into a stream of rapid Czech. They could not understand much of what she said, but they heard the words 'Basset Hound' repeatedly.

Her expression now incredulous, the woman replaced the phone in its cradle and showed them to the lift.

"Third floor on your right, 24B."

∼

"MISS PEPE AND MRS... PASSOLINA?" A SMILING YOUNG WOMAN made a few attempts to pronounce Etta's surname correctly. She was holding an incredible number of folders in her arms, but she seemed pleased to receive visitors.

"That's us," Etta confirmed.

The young woman smiled at Leon. "Please, follow me. Vlastimila is waiting for you." She moved down a long white corridor and stopped in front one of the doors.

As they entered, a woman stood up. There was a folder on the desk in front of her along with a sheet of paper on which she had been making notes. She came forward and shook hands with them. Slightly taller than Etta, she had a pleasantly plump figure, grey hair gathered in a simple chignon behind her head and a firm handshake, but the two women could see in her face that she was shaken up and saddened by what had happened to her boss.

She invited them to sit down at a smaller desk in the room.

"Mrs Coleman told me you met Eva Kladivova during the concert."

"We did. Such a charismatic woman could not pass unobserved," said Dora. "She seemed to be a force of nature."

"She was indeed."

"Mrs Coleman told us you'd known her for quite a long time." Dora leant forward encouragingly.

"I've been with her all my working life. We went through some very tough times during Communism, but even Capitalism has its own challenges. There were times she asked us to make quite a few sacrifices when uncertainty struck." She smiled indulgently. "Once, we went for six months without wages..."

"Surely the employees must have resented that?"

"Maybe in the beginning, but they saw that during those six months, Eva was working like a woman possessed. She even slept in the office and we never saw her buying things for herself. In fact, she sold her car to raise money. Eva didn't fire a single one of her employees, and little by little, the company not only found new international clients, but also managed to pay all the wages in arrears. Then two years later, she surprised us with a generous Christmas bonus. We were alive and kicking – the company had made its transition into the Capitalist system and we were there to thrive."

"After speaking to some of your competitors," said Etta, trying for once to be diplomatic, "we wondered if Ms Kladivova was sometimes a bit unfair on her workers, that she might exploit them in order to compete..."

"That's rubbish!" the woman protested vigorously. "On the contrary, Eva Kladivova was greatly admired by most Czech entrepreneurs. I can assure you, 'exploitation' is not a word to use in relation to her, but she did know exactly how much she could ask of her workers and employees. You had to earn your wages to the last koruna, so she was rather demanding, this is true. But she always operated for the good of the company, which by default meant the good of each of her employees, too."

"All the same, she must have made plenty of enemies in her lifetime."

"Indeed, there were people in executive positions who thought they could still do nothing, as they had done under Communism. They resented her success, not realising it was her hard work, her discipline that made all the difference. But may I ask you how you came to be the ones to identify my boss's body?"

Dora told her about their early morning walk on Saturday and how Etta had spotted the elegant red dress and immediately thought of Eva, passing that information on to the police.

"Do you know if they've made any progress?" Dora asked.

"Not really, they don't share any information apart from what we can read in the newspapers, which is all pretty vague and useless."

"Do you have an idea of what might have happened?"

The woman's lips tightened. For the first time, the expression of pain and loss was replaced by something closer to rage.

"No, but I certainly don't believe it was a robbery."

"Why?"

"Because there were people who hated her. Because we've never had a robbery end that badly in Prague city centre. People maybe drink too much and get involved in tussles, but I find it hard to believe that happened to her. Especially considering…"

"Considering what?"

"Considering she had been going to an event with some of the people who despised her the most."

"Other entrepreneurs, you mean?"

"Exactly."

"It strikes me as odd," said Etta, "that Ms Kladivova decided to go drinking with these people, if they all despised each other so much."

"But that was Eva all over," replied Vlastimila. "She never, ever overlooked a chance to network; she was never off duty, always putting the business first."

"So she liked to keep her enemies – the competitors, if you prefer – close to her, then. Competitors like Josef Janda?"

"Yes, him and the like. They always insinuated she had connections who gave her an unfair advantage."

"None of this was true?"

"It was partly true," the woman conceded, "but they were playing exactly the same game. There are times you need people in high places on your side, maybe a politician or two, and she did exactly as they did, only more so. At the end of the day, believe me, it all boiled down to this: she was simply more talented and more hard working than them."

"But there must be a deeper reason than simple envy for someone to go to such extreme lengths. For example, would someone stand to gain financially from her death?"

"I'm sure plenty of people would."

"Mr Janda, for example, would surely benefit from new clients if he was no longer in direct competition with your company."

"Yes, especially as his company is really struggling at the moment."

"Struggling?" asked Etta in surprise.

"Yes, he lost a big customer to us recently, and he doesn't have a big enough portfolio of clients to make up for this loss. Eva structured our company so that we would never depend heavily on any one client, something she was very proud of..." and it was obvious from the way Vlastimila held her head that she was just as proud.

Etta and Dora looked at each other. Would a company's future be enough motive for a person to kill? Especially one as ethical as Janda. But how much of his image was genuine? What if he had met them after killing Eva Kladivova and simply played his part wonderfully well, pretending to be the concerned employer who would never exploit his workers?

Etta let the swirl of thoughts take over. Luckily, Dora came in with a pertinent question.

"What will happen to the company now?"

"Ha!" Vlastimila said, jerking her head sharply in defiance and anger. "You would never guess – that's the irony of it all." The two women looked at her in surprise. "I'm not sure whether you're acquainted with Mr Egon Zima – he was present at the concert, too."

"Yes, we met him. Isn't he Ms Kladivova's ex-husband?"

"He is. Eva's solicitor has already informed us she left everything to him. Apart from a few charity donations and legacies to me and other long-standing employees, the entire company, her properties, her money – it all goes to him."

"Goodness!" cried the two women in unison, their shock plain to hear.

"Was this known?" asked Etta, the first to recover from her surprise.

"*I* didn't know," and it was clear from the emphasis that if Vlastimila Vodova didn't know, no one else had the right to know.

"Do you think Mr Zima knew?"

"Probably, which would explain why he did what he did."

Etta gasped. "You think it was Mr Zima who killed her? Is that what the police say?"

"The police don't say anything."

"Who did you believe Ms Kladivova had left her company to?"

Vlastimila's face flushed. "I'd never given it a thought."

"You must have done if you're now surprised she left everything to her former husband."

"Maybe I thought she'd create a trust, or give us employees a little more. And then there's Brother Benedikt... maybe I'd expected Eva to be more generous with him and the church. Believe me, if you worked for her, you wouldn't have too much time to think of who might benefit from her death. I thought she'd outlive me anyway."

"But you cannot be much older than her."

"Her vitality made her younger, and definitely stronger. No, believe me, I never thought I'd survive her."

"And Brother Benedikt – is he the monk at Břevnov Monastery?"

"He is."

"Why would you expect your boss to be generous with him and the church?"

"They were quite close in the past, and since Eva had no immediate family..."

"How was she close to Brother Benedikt?" Etta said, raising her eyebrows.

"Not in a personal sense!" the woman cried, offended. "Of course not! But I believe he had been involved in the resistance, and Eva admired him for that."

"I see," said Etta, almost disappointed. "Did she tend to be generous with donations?"

"She did her share," but from Vlastimila's tone, the two women knew the interview was over.

On the threshold, Dora turned to ask one last question. "Did Ms Kladivova keep in touch with Marketa Ciprova?"

"Marketa Ciprova? I don't recall her name."

"She was a nurse at the Embassy during the time of the Velvet Revolution."

"Eva didn't really have much contact with the Embassy. She was there a few times during the revolution – it was very difficult to gain information otherwise – but no, I don't remember her mentioning the name Marketa Ciprova."

~

OUTSIDE, ETTA AND DORA DECIDED NOT TO CATCH THE NEXT TRAM back, instead walking around the Karlin district, a former industrial area with factories now housing offices and new companies, as well as wineries and independent galleries. In the large tree-lined street, there were Art Nouveau buildings and plenty of cafés and restaurants. To Leon's satisfaction, they discovered that Karlínské náměstí was more of a park than a square and he was eager to explore new ground and mark it as if it was his own private property, leaving the two women free to chat.

"Christine was right to suggest we speak to her."

"Yes, she gave us at least three leads," Etta agreed.

"Three?"

"Think about it."

"Well, she seems to think the killer is Ms Kladivova's ex-husband. It seems very sad that there should be such animosity between two people who were once in love, but at the same time, it is so common. Especially as he will inherit all her wealth..."

"Yes, the killer is most likely in her inner circle," Etta said in approval. Dora's skills as a detective were definitely improving – at least she wasn't trying to proclaim everyone she knew as innocent any more.

"But she also mentioned the great rivalry between Ms Kladivova and Mr Janda, and the fact he'd lost at least one important customer to her – a customer who was essential to his business."

"That's correct. With Ms Kladivova no longer around, he can surely win that client back, and claim a greater market share. And the recent conference would have been the ideal place to start."

"But I can't see who the third suspect is," Dora admitted.

"You're already there!" Etta looked triumphant. "What if they were in it together?"

"Goodness!" Dora cried, looking at her friend with unconditional admiration.

"The two of them make plans after the concert, then on the way home, they pretend to go their separate ways when they say goodbye to Mr Smolak, but retrace their steps. It would be far easier for two men to commit the crime – one to make sure no one was around while the other stabbed the poor woman and threw the body from the bridge."

"Oh, the poor woman indeed! And to think, Mr Janda seems such a kind, sensitive man..."

"I see. So you'd prefer Mr Zima to be the murderer?"

"I'd prefer this thing not to have happened at all."

"So very Dora-ish," Etta said with a dismissive sniff.

"You don't think Mr Smolak might have played a part in it too?"

"Certainly not!" Etta stopped so abruptly that Leon had to jump back as the leash pulled him to a sudden halt. "Well actually, that is an interesting hypothesis. What if the three of them had planned it all?"

"What if," Dora jumped in, "that expression you saw on Ms Eva Kladivova's face was a moment of realisation? With all three men in the room, she had a glimpse of what was going to happen..."

"But still she went drinking with them?" Etta contended.

"More often than not, we ignore our premonitions. Modern life and school teach us to be rational..."

"But in that case, why would Mr Smolak want her dead?" Etta wondered.

"We never asked Vlastimila about Mr Smolak..."

"Maybe Ms Kladivova did something to upset him in the past."

"And he came all the way from the States to take his revenge, almost 30 years after the fact?" Even Dora's imagination could not stretch that far.

"I admit, it sounds a bit implausible," Etta said with a certain regret. It had seemed such a good theory, three murderers conspiring, but real life tended to be much more mundane than that.

Dora nodded. She admired the way her friend's brain worked, and Etta knew that – Etta felt sure that had she suggested a Martian had come down to Earth to stab Ms

Kladivova, Dora would have believed her entirely. Strangely, it felt good to know there was at least one person on the planet who trusted her, no matter what. It was a new feeling for Etta – most of her relationships had been pugnacious rather than admiring.

But there was another strange thing that had happened in the past year, since the two women had decided to share their home: Etta had learned to trust Dora. The apparent people pleaser, the woman who looked at the world through rose-tinted glasses – there was much more to Dora than that. There was much in Dora that Etta wished she had known before.

She slid her arm through her friend's and asked joyfully, "Don't you think we deserve a proper lunch today?"

"We have our sandwiches with us."

"Bugger the sandwiches!"

"Don't we have to save for the rest of the trip?"

"We're not going to have afternoon tea at The Savoy! We're in a less touristy area of Prague than usual, so I'm sure we can afford to splash out. Especially as we have to sit down and plan our next moves."

Leon barked in approval, looking forward to a hearty goulash.

14

A HOSTILE NEIGHBOURHOOD

"Hello, Mr Smolak, fancy meeting you here," said Etta in mock surprise as she walked past the Embassy with Dora and Leon.

"Mrs Fletch… I beg your pardon, my Italian friends. How are you?"

"We're on our way home after a walk in Petřín park. Leon is rather fond of it."

"It seems to me he wants to go back," said Mr Smolak, pointing at the hound who was showing them his bum, his long body, from the tip of his nose to the tip of his tail, poised and ready to head in the direction of the park.

The liars, Leon thought. They had not even taken him to the park yet; they had just been standing facing the Embassy, waiting to ambush this foolish man who didn't seem to see through their subterfuge. And now they were clearly determined to talk to him for ages and waste time instead of going in search of the prettiest of she-Bassets.

Oh Guendaline, you're making the life of this poor guy so miserable, yet so worth living.

"Ah Leon, he's never had enough," said Etta, falling into step beside Smolak. "But what about you? Have you finished your work with the roadshow?"

"No, not yet. I had to meet with the Ambassador, and later, I am due to go to dinner with some of his guests, so I will stay in Prague tonight before heading on to Bratislava tomorrow. I'd love to invite you to join us for dinner, but I fear it would be very boring for you. They will just talk about semiconductors and steel bars and profit margins and competition from Eastern Asia..."

"You're right, it would be way over our heads," said Dora, laughing.

"How about a beer on the island of Kampa before I have to go to dinner? You could fill me in on your progress."

"Our progress?" asked Etta as innocently as Pinocchio.

"Yes, I'm sure you've managed to catch the killer in the past couple of days, just to show the police how stupid they are."

"Mr Smolak!" said Etta seriously. "We're here on holiday."

Their conversation stopped abruptly as they realised Dora was not walking with them. Leon was exercising his right to civil disobedience; his bum glued to the pavement, he was refusing to move an inch in any direction other than Petřín Park.

"I don't think he approves of our drinking plan," said Mr Smolak, smiling over to Dora. She was alternately sweet-talking and tugging at the dog.

"Please, pass me the leash," said Mr Smolak. He let it hang loose as he addressed Leon. "I thought you, young chap, would be up for a beer and a bite to eat. They say 6pm is the best time to catch the prettiest she-dogs, and owners, in Kampa park. If I were you, I wouldn't waste time my time in Petřín."

Miraculously, Leon got up and followed the man.

"How did you do that?" asked Etta and Dora in unison. Mr Smolak winked at them.

"Men's talk," he replied.

∼

THEY SAT AT AN OUTSIDE TABLE, PRAGUE'S BEST BEER IN THEIR glasses, and Mr Smolak asked them again what they were up to.

"Don't tell me you've just been touring around as I won't believe you."

The two women filled him in on what they had learned at Eva's office.

"Mr Zima is inheriting everything? Good for him! I wonder if he knew anything about it before Eva's unfortunate death. I don't think his company is in good shape – my impression is that he didn't attract the interest of many US firms during the conference."

"Why is that?"

"He doesn't tick the right boxes. The demand is for high-quality products or components; specifications are getting tougher to meet nowadays..."

"While Ms Kladivova..."

"Eva Kladivova operated in a totally different sector, but more to the point, she was a totally different kind of entrepreneur. From what I've heard, she was a much sought-after partner for most companies. So, you've managed to find a motive for the murder, and most likely a suspect."

"Actually, two," said Dora.

"Two?"

"Mr Janda will also benefit from her death, albeit indirectly. Recently, one of his company's important customers left him for Ms Kladivova. If Mr Zima decides to live off the money he will inherit, or if he doesn't lead the company with the same efficiency as his former wife, Mr Janda will be free of his fiercest rival."

"Wow, I'm impressed. Any more suspects or clues?"

"Well, there's a third possibility," whispered Dora, her voice low and mysterious, ramping up the suspense.

"There is?" The man responded in kind; it was obvious he was enjoying the conversation.

Dora paused momentarily before the big reveal. "The two of them could have acted together."

"Goodness me! I don't know what's more diabolical: that two men could have conspired to commit murder, or that you even thought of such a possibility."

"Have you heard any more from the police?" Etta asked.

"Yes. They said they're on the case, but they won't disclose much. Surely, they must know about the inheritance and the business competition, so I would assume they're investigating both men. But maybe they haven't yet thought about a conspiracy between the two. That, I reckon, requires a degree of imagination, and I'm not sure the police have much. But if that's what happened, they will get there eventually."

Maybe it was the beer, maybe the friendly atmosphere, more likely a combination of the two, but Dora went for audacity.

"Well, the conspiracy, if there is one, might have involved three rather than two players."

"You're blowing my mind! Who's the third party?"

Etta glared at her friend. Dora went redder than the rooftops of Prague. Mr Smolak caught the exchange of glances and understood.

"I see. The three of us went for a drink with Eva Kladivova and it was no chance meeting – we set a trap for her. Three against one. Rather unfair odds, even against a strong-willed woman such as she was…"

"I'm sorry," said Dora, still blushing. "We were just thinking of all possible hypotheses…"

"Fair enough. I guess like the police, you cannot exclude anyone. In the beginning, at least. Nothing personal, I hope?"

"Oh no, absolutely," Dora reassured him with a big smile, "nothing personal."

"And what's your next move?"

"We haven't planned anything yet," Etta replied bluntly. "We might just be a couple of tourists for a few days."

"Until your hunch takes you somewhere else."

"Or not. As you said, the police are on the case, and if everything is straightforward, it shouldn't take them much longer to get to the murderer."

"True," said the man, yawning. "Not all crimes are as full of twists as they are in mystery stories. Reality can be far more boring."

To Dora's relief, they moved on to more mundane subjects, chatting about Prague, Mr Smolak's life in the United States, what he missed about the land of his birth and what he enjoyed about his new country. Then they parted, Mr Smolak regretting that he wouldn't be able to be at the Embassy for their visit on Monday.

"But don't get yourself into trouble. And if you have a sudden inspiration, give me a ring. Even an old man like me can be some good against a murderer."

"Will do," Dora replied meekly, feeling ashamed of having suspected a man who'd already saved their lives once.

~

THEY WALKED AROUND KAMPA PARK, LEON LOOKING OUT FOR Guendaline.

"Mr Smolak is right," said Etta. "The police may well be on the right track this time. But there's just one thing bothering me..."

"Marketa?" guessed Dora.

"Exactly. Let's give her a ring." But again, the phone went straight to voicemail.

"The meeting!" cried Dora.

"What meeting?"

"Don't you remember Mr Janda asking Marketa for her phone number so they could meet up while he was in Prague?"

"Butter my butt and call me a biscuit! How could I forget? So maybe he called her, arranged to meet, and then he did her some harm – or worse."

"Unless she's really at her cousin's house."

"True. Let's not get carried away – the beer isn't helping. We must proceed with method and caution."

It was at that moment that Leon saw the tip of a tail in the crowd ahead of them. He pulled so energetically that both method and caution vanished into thin air as the two women were dragged along, pushing unlucky passers-by out of the way. The Basset only stopped when he realised the tip of the tail actually belonged to a nasty beagle who, on spotting Leon, barked and growled like a whole army of dogs ready to go hunting.

"Calm yourself," Leon sneered, walking past with head and tail held high, pretending total indifference, two out-of-breath women following behind. Then they were back on Nerudova and it wasn't even seven o'clock yet.

"Shall we call at Marketa's house once more?"

"Why not?"

The trio crossed the large square in front of the castle and walked down Nový Svět, quainter than ever in the soft light of sunset. They stopped at the building with the lamb sign and rang the bell, but just as they'd feared, no one opened the door. They tried to peep through the net curtains, but couldn't see much.

A voice addressed them from across the road. The man spoke in Czech first, but when he realised they were foreign visitors, he switched to harshly accented English.

"Are you looking for someone?"

"Our friend, Marketa," Etta said, recognising the man she had seen in the café on their first visit to the nurse's home.

"She left to see her family. An emergency, I believe," he said.

"So we've heard. But have you actually spoken to her since she left?"

"Tuesday morning, I saw her with her luggage. I stopped to ask if she was OK and she told me why she had to leave for a while."

"Thank you for letting us know," Dora said.

"I saw you looking through the windows and I wanted to make sure you weren't thieves. There're plenty of them in Prague, which used to be such a law-abiding city!" the man grumbled.

"Do you live nearby?"

"Yes, I'm in the neighbourhood." But he didn't point to any of the buildings. Instead, he stood in the middle of the cobbled road, looking at them suspiciously as if determined to wait there until they left.

"We've been trying to call her on the phone, but she hasn't replied to our messages..."

"Maybe she doesn't want to be bothered," the man answered dryly without moving a muscle.

The fur on Leon's back bristled. He recognised the aggression in the man's body language, a sentinel guarding his territory, but Leon had been made welcome in that nice woman's house and had received some very good snacks, too. Nový Svět was as much his territory as the old man's.

"Pull that dog away," Etta told Dora. "I don't think we'll learn anything more here."

Leon did not want to concede ground to the man, but when Dora floated the possibility that Guendaline might be on her way home right now, he turned fiercely. Stopping to mark a tuft of grass next door, he kicked the ground with his back legs as if he were a huge, ferocious bull ready to attack. After all, to march through life, you have to be a great pretender.

As they passed the house next door, Dora caught sight of a face just behind the curtains. But she waited until they reached the end of the road before speaking.

"Did you see her?"

"Who?"

"Marketa's neighbour. She was spying from the window."

"Yes. She must be a right gossip behind that scaredy-cat face."

"Indeed, she looked very scared."

"That's what I said."

"No, I didn't mean nervous like last time we called. Today she looked... terrified."

"Are you sure you haven't drunk too much beer?"

"Not at all. I only had a small one, and we've had a good walk since."

"Our resistance to alcohol is building day by day. We will impress our Scottish friends when we guzzle all their whisky, I'm sure..."

"Etta, I'm not joking! She looked *really* scared, I can't get her expression out of my mind. And did you notice, she said she had heard noises on Tuesday evening? But the awful man said it was early in the morning when he saw Marketa leaving..."

Etta stopped in her tracks. "Miss Dorotea Rosa Pepe, that's very true." She looked at her friend in admiration and Dora's cheeks blushed with pleasure.

"Do you think it's important?"

"Of course, it means one of them is lying."

"But who?"

"Much as I want it to be the nasty old man, it has to be the neighbour. Remember, we'd already had a message from Marketa telling us she'd had to leave town by Tuesday evening. But why? And if it wasn't Marketa the neighbour heard, then who was it?

"We need to call a halt to these many uncertainties. Tomorrow, we're going to see this thing through once and for all. And I know exactly where our first port of call will be, dog included."

15

A TRAIN RIDE AND A TOUR GUIDE

A delightful train ride took Etta, Dora and Leon from Prague to Karlštejn, through countryside brightened by trees in full bloom. The station they arrived at was small, white and neat, and once they left it, there was no need to ask for directions. All the passengers were marching the same way, over the bridge crossing the Berounka River and through the small town with café tables outside in the sunshine.

The town itself was no more than a bunch of red roofs emerging from the luxuriant vegetation. On the sides of the streets were all sorts of shops, kiosks and stalls, selling everything from fruit to handmade knives and tools for gardening, Bohemian crystals to newspapers, postcards, soft drinks, kebabs and other fast food.

Then from the treetops, the castle emerged in the distance. Its tall rectangular tower, pointed roofs with grey slate tiles, its turrets, ramparts, battlements, walls and many chimneys seemed to spring out from the forest like an illustration in a fairy tale book.

"Aww!" gasped Dora in her trademark style, standing still as a statue, her hands clasped to her breast. Etta was quick to grab Leon's leash before he decided to take them on a long detour through the forest, but the dog too was looking ecstatically at the castle. Not that he was thinking what an architectural jewel it was, nor about how people had lived there in the past; his mind was on Guendaline and how nice it would have been to visit this place with her. Or even better, they could live in the castle together: a huge forest around them for their daily gallops, plenty of bipeds to serve Their Majesties with the best food ever and pamper and groom them, and maybe a tribe of gorgeous puppies to educate and take care of.

"The tourists will think we're street artists being living statues and asking for money," complained Etta, looking at her dazzled companions. But it still took some minutes before the biped of the two could finally speak.

"Oh Etta, it's just like in the pictures, so lovely and romantic."

"You expected the Tourist Board to use fake pictures and have visitors come all this way simply to find some anonymous ruins?"

"No! I meant that when you see something looking so good in the pictures, you almost fear the real thing might not be quite as perfect... I'm not sure I can explain myself. But look at Leon, I'm sure he feels exactly as I do."

The dog, his head tilted, was imagining returning from the forest after having fought against a fearsome dragon and won. Guendaline was running up to him, tears in her eyes, fearing her brave Napoleon might have been injured in the dangerous battle.

"My hero!" she'd cry, her eyes full of Basset-love.

"It was bad enough you suffering from these attacks of inertia, but I never imagined you would infect the dog, too."

"It's not a disease; it's just good to be grateful for the chances we have to visit such amazing places..."

"We're not here as tourists," Etta answered bluntly. As much as Dora was happy to pass for another holidaymaker, Etta took pride in visiting the place on official business. Even when... they weren't. "We're here to find out about Marketa's cousin."

"That's absolutely true!" Dora agreed, disentangling her

hands from each other. After having gently woken Leon up from his romantic dreams, the two women took to the road, passing yet more restaurants, bars and souvenir shops.

∽

ONCE THEY WERE INSIDE THE CASTLE'S DEFENCE WALLS, THE TWO women found themselves at the end of an extremely long queue. Etta left Dora to her hand clasping and wowing, and knotted Leon's leash to a bench, determined to make sure she'd return to as many companions as she had left. Then she moved past the line of people until a man in the queue addressed her in English.

"Hey, where do you think you're going?"

"Just getting some information."

"Is that an Italian accent?"

"That's none of your business."

"It is, and I'll tell you what: it's time for you Italians to learn to respect rules and not push in."

"And it's time you Yankees learned to keep your opinions to yourself. I'm not here to visit the castle, I need to get information."

The man's wife tried to silence her husband, but he was still grumbling. "If we were in the States, they would throw her outside, but in this country…"

Etta moved on, careless of raising protests from the queue. But when she reached the front, she discovered there were just ticket booths; nowhere to ask for information.

"Where do I get information on the guided tour?" she asked a nearby security guard. The man directed her to the ticket booths. "I don't need a ticket, just to ask for information."

The man showed her a large poster half in English, half in Czech explaining the types of tickets available, their cost and length of the tour.

"I don't need information about tickets, I need to speak to someone in the office. It's urgent."

For the first time, the man spoke in tentative English. "Have appointment?"

"I do."

"Who with?"

Etta was lost for a fraction of a second. "The director."

"Name?" the man insisted.

Etta muttered a few consonants, then finished with emphasis on OVA.

"Name again?"

"I'm not sure how you pronounce it in Czech, but it's something like TzprtzsctOVA."

The man looked at her with a cold smile. "No, not here. Need to go in the queue." He showed her the long line of people.

Etta sighed and tried to join the queue near the front, but some extremely rude people told her to get to the back.

"Learn to respect the elderly, I'm over sixty…" but as she said that, she silenced herself. Not even queue jumping was worth mentioning her age for, let alone pretending she was a fragile, needy old woman.

Such a stupid move! she reprimanded herself.

"There she is," said the American man when he saw her passing. "They've sent her to the back of the queue. As I said, the Czechs are great people."

"Shut up, moron, or I'll send my mafia cousin to cut off your ears, as well as anything you keep in pairs under your belly."

His wife paled and forbade her husband to reply. Then a couple ahead of them invited Etta to take their place and they'd go to the back of the queue, an invitation Etta didn't turn down. With a grin, she silently thanked her imaginary mafia cousin for allowing her to skip a boring wait in a long queue.

Mind you, it was quite a while before she was finally facing the ticket seller. Without even looking up, he asked, "Do you have a booking?"

"Of course not, otherwise I wouldn't be here. But I'm not here for a ticket; I'm looking for a woman who does guided tours."

"Which ticket do you want?"

"I don't want a damn ticket."

"Basic, exclusive or tower view tour? The first two are guided only."

"Basic."

"Sold out for today."

"Exclusive."

"Sold out for today."

"Tower view does not come with a guide?"

"No. So, what ticket?"

"I need a guided tour for today!"

"You can get your ticket and if someone doesn't turn up, you can take their place. If there's no place today, you need to return tomorrow and I'll book you in then. Do you understand?"

"More than you ever did in your entire lifetime."

"So, what tour?"

"The basic tour."

"You won't see the Lapidarium, the Great Tower and the Chapel of the Holy Cross."

"Will there at least be a few bare walls?"

"That's how many tourists describe their tour after the visit. So don't be disappointed, I did warn you."

"The exclusive tour, then."

"How many tickets?"

"Two."

"That's 1,040 koruna."

"What?"

"One thou-sand-and-for-ty-ko-ru-na." The man enunciated the words, pointing at the amounts showing on the cash till display.

"There must be a mistake. I only asked for two, not twenty tickets."

The ticket seller sighed. The man behind Etta in the queue sighed. The whole line of people sighed.

"Each exclusive ticket costs 520 koruna; 520 times two equals one thousand and forty."

Once she'd reluctantly paid for the tickets, Etta was told to wait in the courtyard for the tour to start, and then ask the guide if there was room for her and her friend, too. Etta returned to Dora, who had thankfully emerged from her trance and was chatting with a young blonde woman.

Isn't she the lassie from Australia we met in front of the Lennon wall? Etta thought. It had to be her, because Leon was being particularly affectionate and submissive, something he reserved for people he had already met. Especially charming young women.

"Good morning," said the charming young woman.

"Hello," Etta replied. "I guess this is a must-see for visitors to Prague."

"It is. Did you manage to get your tickets?"

"Not sure, we're on a waiting list."

"I hope you will manage to get inside…" but her face wasn't that enthusiastic.

"You've been in?"

"Yes, I've just finished a tour. I booked my ticket in advance."

"Was it worth the money?"

"Well, I don't want to spoil your visit, but as is often the case, the best part of this castle visit is the outside." The woman winked at her.

"I knew it! And I've just had 1,000 koruna extorted from me!"

"That's the long tour; I guess it'll be much better than the basic one I did. But it lasts a couple of hours and I want to hike around, too."

"Two hours!" cried Etta. She hated guided tours; unless you struck lucky, most guides were just fed-up employees, counting the minutes to the end of their working day, speaking like robots, resorting to incomprehensible words whenever you asked them something to make you feel ignorant and worthless.

"How lovely," chirped Dora who, of course, adored guided

tours. "Thanks to those generous guides, we will get to know all the secrets and legends of the castle."

"Generous, my eye! Two hours per tour means we'll have to hang around here for more than four hours. And, of course, dogs are not allowed inside." Etta gave Leon a dirty look, implying he should feel the shame and guilt of being a canine. But he was blissfully happy, stretched in a beam of sunlight, legs in the air, enjoying the gentle hands of the Australian woman tickling his belly. Life could be a wonderful thing at times.

"If they squeeze you in for the next tour, I'd love to take Leon for a walk. I will be back here in a couple of hours. If he wants to come along, that is."

Leon wagged his tail and looked at the young woman's fresh slightly freckled face, her blue eyes as deep as the ocean. He could get lost in those eyes.

～

ALTHOUGH ONE PERSON DIDN'T SHOW UP FOR THE NEXT TOUR, IT was a difficult business to convince the guide that a group of 17 rather than 16 would not spoil the visit completely. Luckily, the nasty American man was not in the group, and the others said it would be a shame not to allow the two women to join them.

"OK," said the guide, somewhat resentfully. "But if the tour isn't as good as you expected, it's not my fault, it's your responsibility. It has been determined by experts that 16 is the optimum number to get the best out of the visit, but oh no. You know best…"

"It's only one extra person," said a woman with a strong French accent, trying to appease the irritated guide. "We're not doubling the number of visitors."

"Yes, but the tour is meant for 16. These things have been carefully researched, studied and organised for enhancing the highlights of the visit."

The woman made a typically Gallic "Pfft!" sound. Etta loved her in that moment, but knew better than to get carried away.

"Dora, you'd better try to soften that jobsworth up," she whispered as the tour finally started. "If I do it, I'm sure either she or I will have to leave the castle, if not the Czech Republic."

Before they entered the first room, the guide informed them that neither photos nor videos were allowed.

"Of course," Etta couldn't resist a bit of sarcasm, "photos are allowed in the Vatican Museum, where they only have a few Raffaellos, Michelangelos, the history of humankind in art. But what's that compared to Karlštejn?"

"You can take photos at the Louvre," added the French woman, winking at Etta.

"And the British museum," said a man with a posh English accent, "where you're actually allowed in without a ticket."

"These are the rules," the tour guide replied, determined to quash the mutiny and deciding it was going to be a long day.

16

KARLŠTEJN CASTLE

The tour, rather boring at the beginning, became more interesting when they visited the two chapels that were steeped in the atmosphere of the past. Unfortunately – or fortunately, depending on your point of view – Dora didn't have much time to enjoy what she saw as Etta kept on hassling her to sweet talk the guide, if that were possible with such a sour-faced woman.

"It won't be easy after all your sarcasm and jibes," Dora protested.

"If there's anyone who can do it, it's you," Etta replied. "You could save the world with your honeyed words."

Dora looked at her friend with a dubious expression, wagging her finger at her as if Etta were a naughty child. Then they grinned at each other.

Dora moved over to the guide and started to ask her a few pertinent questions. The woman could finally show off her knowledge and competence thanks to an attentive student, and her face gradually lost the sour expression it had been wearing since this rebellious group had insisted on flouting the 16 people rule. Then Dora moved on to phase B: empathy. As they were walking from one room to the next, she asked the woman what life as a tour guide at the castle was like.

"It certainly requires a lot of energy to deal with such a heterogeneous bunch of people. They come from all over the place and their behaviour at times is... well... it crosses the lines a little."

The woman was clearly overjoyed to have such a sympathetic listener and launched into a stream of national stereotypes. The Italians – present company excepted, of course – were so incurably Italian, the French intolerably French, the Russians – when a Russian dared to visit after what they had done to the Czech Republic – had no sense of discipline and respect whatsoever. The Americans were naïve – she was sure they envisaged Karl the Emperor as a superhero, wearing a blue costume and a flowing red cloak and flying – still alive, of course – past the castle ramparts. The woman, it seemed, had a derogatory opinion on every single nationality on earth, including the ungrateful Slovaks. In fact, from her point of view, they were the worst of them all.

A little bored of this diatribe, Dora moved through Phase B, wondering out loud how tired the woman must become doing such a responsible job. Another flood of words issued forth from the guide as she explained to Dora how hard her life was, how much was demanded of her, how little she was paid for the huge number of things she had to do.

"If I forget to close up one of the rooms properly, for example, you can be sure at least one tourist will sneak in. Can you see what a weight of responsibility that is? All on one person's shoulders."

Dora shook her head in sympathy, as if the woman were an overworked miner transporting tonnes of stones on her back. This was the exact moment to strike. The victim was ready for Phase C.

"You know what? We met a woman in Prague whose cousin

works here. She's a guide like you, so I wonder if you know her. I bet her life is as tough as yours."

"Almost all of us have a relative who lives in Prague. Do you know her name?"

"Not exactly, but her cousin in Prague is a retired nurse who used to work at the US Embassy. We were invited to a concert at the National Theatre last week, and during the refreshments that followed, she mentioned how much she loved to visit her cousin here in Karlštejn."

"The US Embassy?" the guide repeated, looking at Dora for the first time as if she could be someone important. "What's the name of the nurse?"

"Marketa Ciprova."

"Oh Marketa, yes! She's Anne's cousin – how did I not think of her straight away? Dear Marketa, she's such a kind woman. Mind you, she doesn't understand how difficult it is to be a guide compared to simply being a nurse. After all, when you're dealing with sick people, they just accept your authority, whereas we deal with healthy people who test our patience on a daily…"

Dora wondered for a second how long she would have to keep listening to a woman who wished that all the world was lying sick in bed so she could assert her authority. Even Dora, with her endless patience, decided that she had had enough.

"So, about Anne. I've heard *she's* not too well."

"She's unwell?" the woman repeated, looking a little puzzled.

"That's what I heard…"

"I don't think so. She's not called in sick at work and she looked fine to me…"

"Really?" Dora said. "Is she on duty today?"

"Of course she is."

"Are you sure?"

"Yes, it's a working day."

"But as I understood it, Marketa had come to visit her because she had been taken ill."

"Well, I don't know about Marketa being in Karlštejn, but Anne's most certainly at work. Maybe it's her husband who's ill."

"Does he have a history of bad health?"

"Fit as a fiddle, as far as I know."

"Maybe I misunderstood what Marketa said. But I'd love to say hello to her cousin – it seems almost as if I know her after Marketa told me all about her country cottage, and you have been good enough to describe what a tour guide's life is like."

"Once the tour is over, I will look for her. Or if she's on a tour, I'll ask her to get in touch with you as soon as she's free."

"That would be great! I'll leave you my phone number so she can give me a call. I'll stay in the area after the tour."

As all things, good and bad, come to an end, so did the tour. The guide signalled to Dora to wait, and moments later, she was back.

"Anne will finish her tour in about 15 minutes. I sent her a message, asking her to meet you in here. She'll be wearing her guide's uniform and a badge with her name on it, so you can't miss her. And if you ever happen to come to Karlštejn again, you're very welcome to call on me."

"I will certainly do that, dear," said Dora, giving the woman a large tip under Etta's disapproving gaze. "You have to pay your informants, you never know when you might need them again," she told her friend as soon as the guide was out of earshot.

~

Etta and Dora just had time to get themselves a refreshing drink – no beer this time – and sit down to rest their ears after 120 minutes of guided tour when a woman, her face pointed like a vixen's, her hazel eyes twinkling, her manner lively, came forward to greet them.

"Are you Marketa's friends?" she asked.

"We are," answered Dora, introducing herself and Etta, shaking hands and exchanging pleasantries.

"So, how is Marketa?" Anne asked, laughing. "What's this sudden trip all about?"

"What sudden trip?"

"Sorry, I thought you knew about it."

"No, we don't. Marketa left us a message saying she'd had to come here to Karlštejn as you had suddenly been taken ill."

"No way! She isn't here and I'm as fit as a fiddle. The message I got from her said she'd finally booked herself on a group touring Europe."

"Oh!" said Etta.

"Ah!" said Dora.

"It's a long-term dream of hers," Anne said. "The only thing is..."

Dora and Etta, hanging on her every word, squirmed impatiently in their seats.

"The only thing is?" Etta repeated to encourage the woman to complete her sentence.

"The only thing is she hasn't called me once since she left, nor replied to my messages."

"Isn't that worrying?"

"A little, but on the other hand, as my husband says, maybe she's found a kindred spirit and is holidaying with him and doesn't want to be bothered."

"The strange thing is," said Dora, showing Anne the message she had received from Marketa, "that she told us she was coming here because her cousin was sick. We thought that meant you."

"And when we had dinner with her," continued Etta, "she seemed rather proud of her independence, and that she had never relied on a man."

"This *is* weird." Anne frowned.

"Does she have another cousin or family member here?"

Anne didn't reply at first. Instead, she read the message on

Dora's phone again and again. Then she sat, or rather collapsed, on the bench beside them.

"No, she has no other family but my husband and me here in Karlštejn. It's not like her to say something that is so clearly untrue – saying one thing to you, people she's only just met, and something totally different to me. It doesn't make sense."

"Normally, would you keep in touch between one visit and the next?"

"Absolutely, we phone each other at least once a week, usually twice, and send messages in between. That's why I was surprised to receive her message telling me her plans, and then nothing further."

Dora and Etta asked if Anne had heard what had happened to Eva Kladivova.

"Of course I heard the news. It's not every day that someone gets killed in Prague city centre like that, but I thought it was a robbery that ended badly. That's what the police and the press are saying."

"We think there might be more to it than that." Etta told Anne how a mystery man had tried to attack them after their visit to Marketa on Monday.

"I wonder if it's something to do with the Embassy, again..."

"Again?"

The woman sighed like someone recalling events they would rather have forgotten about.

"Yes, when Marketa started to work for the Embassy, she was in one of those clandestine groups fighting for freedom of thought. She was never one to bow down to totalitarianism and she wasn't the kind of woman to keep quiet and wait for things to change by themselves. Oh no, she had to get involved."

"But those times are gone. Why would the past bother her decades after the Velvet Revolution?"

The woman was taken aback. "I don't know, but I can't think of any other reason why she could be in danger. That was the only time people might have wished her dead, and I guess that is why they took her on at the US Embassy. She was trusted by the revolutionaries and could deliver news from one side to the other. As officially she was simply a nurse, there was nothing the Communists could do. And the Embassy provided her with some security – it wouldn't do for her to disappear or be threatened while she was employed there."

"Who was she in touch with at the time?"

"The Charter 77 people and some others running clandestine magazines. She would use the printer at the hospital or the Embassy or wherever to print and distribute what the rebels were writing."

"Is she still in touch with any of these people?"

"I don't think so. Those times are gone, people are busy living their lives, and she is not the kind of person who wants to be involved in politics just for the sake of it. She's always looked at that as a chapter of her life, mission accomplished, and now she is happy to enjoy her retirement."

"It can't be such a closed chapter of her life if she has disappeared. No one would wake up all of a sudden and decide both she and Eva Kladivova had to be punished…"

"Do you know if she kept in touch with Ms Kladivova?" Dora asked. Etta nodded in approval at the question.

"Not that I know of. Marketa has never mentioned her to me in all these years…"

"They say Eva Kladivova was also involved with Charter 77, so maybe they collaborated in the past."

"Maybe, but I don't think Ms Kladivova had a very active role in the revolution. Although she 'tolerated' certain activities within her company, like providing shelter and protection."

"Maybe she and Marketa have kept in touch and she just didn't mention it," insisted Dora.

"That'd be strange as they didn't have much in common. Ms Kladivova is… was a successful and rich entrepreneur. But now that I come to think of it, there is at least one person from the past Marketa kept in touch with: Brother Benedikt."

"Oh yes, Marketa mentioned him to us as well – the monk who was sent to the uranium mines…"

"That's him."

"Apparently, he was at Strahov, but he's at another monastery now…"

"At Břevnov, Marketa said on Monday."

"Is he really?" asked Anne. "That's a bit out of town, but it's easy to reach from Prague by tram. Or you could even walk it."

"Before we concentrate too much on the past, are you sure Marketa never mentioned anyone recently who might have wanted to do her harm? Any peril, anything she felt was threatening her?"

"Not at all, but I'll be going to the police and reporting what you've told me and that I can't get in touch with her. They have to do something, she might be in danger."

"Are you going to tell the police here in Karlštejn?" asked Etta.

"Yes, why?"

"Would it be too much of a hassle for you to go to Prague, where they're already investigating Ms Kladivova's death? We tried to explain our concerns at the sudden disappearance of Marketa to the police there, and tell them about the man who attacked us, but they didn't seem to take us seriously. It should be different if a relative expresses the same concerns."

"Yes, you're right, I'd better go to the police in Prague. And while I'm there, I can check Marketa's house."

"Do you have a spare set of keys?"

"I do."

"I'd go to the police first, then to her house later."

"Why?"

"Should the police decide to do something, the forensics will have an easier job if everything in the house has been left untouched."

They exchanged phone numbers with the promise to keep in touch.

~

Outside the castle, Etta and Dora found Leon proudly leading a group of Australians back to where their adventure had started. Sadly, he had not found a dragon to chase, but he had scared a hare who had dared to cross their path.

"And you know?" the young Aussie said. "The path was not perfectly signposted, and Leon took us right where we wanted to go, and back. If we were not this far away from home, he'd be the perfect boyfriend for Augustine, my Bassett back in Melbourne."

Proud as Leon was of the compliment, his heart was already taken.

17

PRAGUE'S SECRET CORNERS

I t was a long, pleasant walk away from the crowds of the Old Town to the Střešovice district. On a Saturday, it seemed the people of Prague were happy to sleep in a little more to start their weekend. Although the two women and one dog were passing along endless roads of unimaginative grey Communist buildings, one looking very much like the next, there was still a lot of greenery around. And thanks to Dora's keen eyes and attentive study of maps, they found some older buildings that used to be family farms, but had now been turned into retirement houses surrounded by orchards, the trees mostly in blossom at that time of the year, and little ponds.

Leon stopped at Vila Kajetánka, a café inside a building that looked like a palace on a pretty pond filled with red fish. A rather unwelcoming waitress served them coffee and had to be asked three times before she brought some water over to the Basset. But no snack.

Dora went to have a look inside the café, which welcomed guests with chandeliers of Bohemian crystal, chequered marble floors, a double staircase going up to the higher levels of the vaulted chambers that were lined with bookshelves, and comfy tables to sit at and enjoy the warmth on a winter afternoon. And sitting inside, facing an empty fireplace as this was *not* a winter afternoon, was Mr Egon Zima, his nose deep in a newspaper.

Dora was tempted to ignore him, but curiosity – and, of course, necessity; weren't they there on a fact-finding mission? – prevailed.

"Mr Zima, what a surprise to find you here!"

The man mumbled a greeting, looking at her with a tired, possibly annoyed face that made it clear he hadn't expected to be found here, a fair way from the city centre.

"I wanted to apologise," said Dora, aware she needed to be a little economical with the truth – something she wasn't fond of.

"What for?"

"For the last time we met. Do you mind if I sit down for a minute? It's a long walk from our accommodation and I don't have the same stamina as I did 10 years back…"

Mr Zima flashed a brief smile and gestured at her to take a seat.

"That's better. What was I saying? Oh yes, please accept our apologies – mine and Etta's. When we met you in Malostranské náměstí the other day, we didn't realise you were so close to Ms Kladivova." Of course, Mr Smolak had already told them that the two had once been married, but there are times in life when you're obliged to tell little lies.

"We were not that close…"

"We'd heard you were once husband and wife."

"That, Ms…"

"Pepe, Miss Dorotea Rosa Pepe, or simply Dora."

"That, Miss Pepe, was back in the nineties. And of the five years we were officially married, we only lived as a husband and wife for two at most."

"That's a short time, even by today's standards."

"Let's just say it was the euphoria of the Velvet Revolution, of owning two businesses that brought us together. We imagined we had the same desire to live in freedom…"

"So what happened?" She asked her questions as only Dora could. Etta would have said Dora spoke with such innocence that people were compelled to reply, and that's exactly how Mr Zima felt.

"Well," he said, opening his arms out and revealing the full shabbiness of his clothes, "I don't know how well you got to know Eva, but she was a strong, ambitious woman. By contrast, I'm a simple man. For her, the liberation was the starting point of a career, launching a winning business, getting rich. For me... I was attracted by the freedom to finally be able to express my own ideas, to discuss them openly with other people. My company has always been a means to an end, a way to put a bit of money aside to do a few other things. Those two visions of life couldn't last long side by side."

Even Dora wondered how truthful this portrait was of Zima as a man disinterested by riches. Was it a ploy to deflect any suspicion of greed away from himself?

"Still, you must have stayed good friends."

The man looked at her intently. It seemed as if he were regarding her as more than just a silly old woman for the first time, maybe even a threat.

"Why do you say that?"

"Well, as is to be expected, all the people interviewed by the police have spoken to one another. And the fact that you have inherited everything from your ex-wife came to light."

"I guess you can't stop people talking. But I didn't think that you, being a mere tourist, would have found that out." It seemed as if he were speaking more to himself than to Dora.

"But as I do know, why do you think she left everything to you?"

"Because Eva had no other family. Or maybe she was simply too busy to change her will. She was certainly not the kind to think about death in general, her own even less."

"So her will didn't come as a surprise?"

The man crumpled the paper he was reading as if that would help him contain his nervousness. "It was a surprise inasmuch as I hadn't given it a thought. But now that I've been informed, I can see it was very Eva-like."

"Apparently, you were bickering when you went out for drinks after the concert." Dora decided it was time to push harder.

"How do you know about that?" Then he shook his head as if he didn't care. "With some people, it doesn't matter how much time has elapsed, you can pick up from exactly where you left the last argument. It was like that with Eva and me. She always had something to hurl at me, and I guess I responded in kind. Now if you don't mind, I've had enough of an interrogation for one day. Pardon me." And with that, he got up, went over to the waitress and paid his bill.

As soon as the man left the café, Dora approached the same cantankerous waitress and asked to settle their bill. Then she ran out to Etta and told her they had to leave, now.

"But we've only just sat down."

"I know, but we need to follow Mr Zima," and she pointed to the man who was climbing up some steps in the park at the back of Vila Kajetánka. Leon sprang up and Etta did the same. Leaving the café, the three of them let Mr Zima get some distance ahead so that he wouldn't realise he was being followed.

At the top of the steps, they found themselves on a wide street. No more grey Communist buildings; these were two- and three-storey houses with big gardens. But Mr Zima seemed to have disappeared.

"Maybe he's gone into one of the houses."

"Leon doesn't think so," Dora replied as the dog pulled her forward onto a winding side street. A romantic villa covered with wisteria and a cast-iron lamp looking like an old-fashioned gaslight stood at the entrance of the little cobbled lane.

"Na Kocourkách?" Etta tried to read the street sign in the difficult Czech language.

"Wow!" Dora cried as her jaw dropped down onto her sternum in total bliss. They were no longer in a city; this was a quaint village where spring was waking up from its long winter sleep. Every single bush and tree was an explosion of colour, the pastel houses so cute you could easily sit there on a little bench next to the gaslight and just stare.

"We can't stand here and dream, not if you want to catch your man!" Etta said. And despite herself, Dora let her romanticism subside and the chase continued.

They were just in time as the man was entering a garden through a gate. Three children came out of the house to greet him, followed by a young blonde woman who hugged him before inviting him inside.

As the door closed behind Zima, the two women were left to contemplate the small garden he had just vacated. It was still beautiful, even though it was in need of maintenance, as was the old building with its scorched yellow façade and chipped stucco columns beside the large wooden door.

"It's badly in need of some work," said Etta.

"But it's so charming!"

"With a bit of money, it will become even more charming. With three children and a pretty wife to take care of, he might not be as content to make do as he pretends. But he'll be content now with all that money pouring down on them."

"Instead of going back to the park, shall we carry on down here for a bit?" said Dora, curious to see more of the little street.

"I agree, but only if you promise you won't drift off into one of those trances of yours: no hand clasping, no ahhs and no wows! Feet solidly on the ground, no levitation allowed."

Dora sighed, wishing she could explain to Etta how her emotions took her by surprise, assaulting her when she least expected it. With a supreme effort, she did as she was asked and didn't let out a single cry, not even at the antique water pump, shaded by a willow tree, nor when the little street climbed up between ivy-covered stone walls, nor when the view opened out on to forget-me-not flowerbeds under a blue-framed window. It was all so lovely; to avoid clasping her hands, she had to put them into her coat pockets and clench her fists, hard. What a difficult exercise!

18

MONASTERIES, MONKS AND BEERS

"That's the Monastery!" Dora cried.

After rows and rows of concrete buildings, the white façade, the red roof and the blue-green bell tower reflecting in a pond surrounded by the most romantic willow trees, a few silver shrubs and the ever-present lilac flowers, stood out proudly.

"Such a sight," she said, forgetting all Etta's commands and clasping her hands in delight.

"Actually, too much of it," Etta replied. The warm and sunny Saturday had brought with it loud music, cheap street food, crowds picnicking on the grass. To her, all it did was ruin the atmosphere of the place irrevocably.

They pushed through the crowd and, to their surprise, found a sanctuary of peace on the other side of the Monastery. The music disappeared; the visitors were fewer and mostly not so loud; everything seemed to be in perfect order. The beautiful St Margaret's Church was closed, but through the glass door at the entrance, Etta and Dora were able to view the rich Baroque interior – along with a priest exiting via a side door.

"Good morning," Etta stopped him. "We're looking for Brother Benedikt."

"He'll be at the Brewery right now, probably busy serving

lunch." As he said this, the priest showed them a paved road between two lawns. There were four buildings scattered around and he pointed to the one that looked like a farmhouse on their left.

"It looks quite busy," said Dora, watching the waiters moving fast between the tables outside.

"We only have a few questions," replied Etta, as ever less mindful of other people's needs.

They passed the beer garden, moving inside the rustic restaurant with its exposed beams, long, crowded communal tables, a large mantelpiece at the bottom of the room and a stone floor. Etta stopped a waiter who had four hot dishes balanced on his arms.

"We're looking for Brother Benedikt."

The man patiently indicated the bar in front of the entrance with a nod of his head. As Etta pushed her way through the crowd, she saw a lanky monk working at the bar. With deep brown eyes and a humorous expression underneath his thick white brows, he seemed to serve every single beer with a laugh and a joke, all in Czech as there seemed to be very few international tourists around.

"What can I serve you, madam?" asked Brother Benedikt, recognising that Etta was a foreigner.

"I'm a friend of Christine Coleman of the US Embassy. My friend and I would like to speak to you."

The man looked around, inviting them to appreciate how busy the restaurant was, and said, "I'd be very happy to talk, but would one of you take my place? Or maybe you'd like to sit down for a nice Czech lunch, and as soon as everyone's stomach is happy with food and drink, I might find someone to take over from me at the bar."

For once, Etta thought better of complaining and did exactly what she was asked.

"We'll sit outside to eat," she announced to Dora, who was overjoyed they would be having lunch in a real Czech restaurant. "It can't be that expensive, if it is run by monks," Etta continued.

"And Benedictines typically grow their own vegetables, so I'm sure the food is all fresh and healthy."

"They certainly cultivate their barley crop," answered Etta, pointing to the numerous glasses being carried all around the room.

They had to wait for a while to find an empty table, where they enjoyed a delicious mushroom soup and shared a large portion of roasted pork served with sour cherries and apple and horseradish sauce. And the traditional cottage cheese dumplings with apple dip and Bohemian flapjacks with blueberries and fresh whipped cream for dessert were even more delicious than their appearance suggested.

Leon put his broken heart to one side to help out with the huge amount of pork, and he thought the meat was divine, especially accompanied by potatoes. But he was not allowed to try any of the beer the two women were drinking, limiting themselves to a small glass each. To their dismay, Czech beer seemed to go down much faster than any other beer they'd tried before.

Maybe it was the satisfying lunch, or the melodic buzzing of the bees; maybe it was the gentle spring air, the long walk or the beer, but when a cheerful voice called out to them, all three were surprised from their daydreams.

"Sorry to wake you up, but I will have to go for prayer later, so this is the best moment for a chat."

While Dora, Etta and Leon squirmed in their places, trying to regain some composure, pretending to have simply been deep in thought and perfectly aware of what was going on around them, the monk took a seat at their table.

"As you know, I'm Brother Benedikt. Did you come here just to visit the Monastery?"

The direct question called for a direct answer.

"No, we have somehow managed to become involved in the

investigations into the death of Ms Kladivova. We were at the theatre for a concert she attended the night she died, and we happened to be passing by when the police found her body the next morning, so we identified it."

"Poor Eva, may God rest her soul." The man looked at them as if he was still unable to believe it. "I read about it in the news... but what can I do for you?"

"After the concert, we had a chance to speak to Marketa Ciprova, the nurse who worked for the Embassy..."

"Dear, energetic, forever optimistic Marketa; she's such a good woman."

"She told us that you knew Eva Kladivova and we wondered if you could help us with a little of her backstory."

"In what respect?"

"Anything that happened in her past that might be significant. Marketa told us that despite her success after the Revolution, she hadn't had an easy life."

"That's true, but I still can't understand why you've come to visit me."

Etta thought about fibbing. She was good at fabricating a story on the spot, but there was something in the monk's eyes that warned her he wouldn't be taken in. He seemed to be the kind of man who could see beyond words to the essence of the matter. And anyway, they needed to trust at least one person, or there would be no way forward in the investigation.

"The day we went to visit Marketa, we were followed and nearly attacked by a stranger. Luckily, a friend of ours spotted the man skulking in the shadows and scared him off."

"Who was he?"

"We don't know, he got away before we were able to find out, although we did see his face. He was no more than mid-twenties, possibly sent by someone else. The next day, we tried to get in touch with Marketa, but we got no answer until the evening when she sent us a brief message saying she was heading out to

Karlštejn as her cousin had been taken ill, making us believe there was some sort of emergency."

"I hope there's nothing seriously wrong with her cousin."

"As a matter of fact, no." Etta told the monk about their visit to Karlštejn and their conversation with Anne. "So while we were thinking she was with her sick cousin, Anne, who is not ill at all, believed she was travelling in Europe, and none of us have received a reply to our messages. Her phone is never on."

"Really?"

Etta nodded gravely and gave him all the details of the different messages they and Anne had received.

"We also spoke to Marketa's neighbour, who confirmed that she had received the same message as ours, but for some reason, she seemed really scared. If Ms Kladivova hadn't been murdered, we possibly wouldn't have taken any notice of this, but in the light of recent events, the sudden disappearance of Marketa has filled us with worry."

"Both women were connected with the Embassy and both were involved in the rebellions in the eighties."

"Basically, we started to wonder…"

"…if Eva's murder and Marketa's disappearance are connected to something that happened in the past rather than in the present, maybe when Shirley Temple Black was the US Ambassador in Prague. Because in the present, as far as we know, Marketa and Ms Kladivova weren't in touch…"

"And we couldn't think of any other link…"

"So you came here to ask me to shed some light on the past?" the monk asked.

The two women nodded. "Marketa mentioned your name and said you were a friend of Mrs Temple Black, the then Ambassador. Then it was Ms Kladivova's secretary who told us she found it strange that her boss had not left you – I mean your church – a larger part of her estate. Instead, it all went to her ex-husband, Egon Zima."

"So as you knew both women, we wondered if you could help us close the circle, as it were."

The monk sat in silence in front of them, then he rose from the table and spoke.

"Let's take a walk. A little fresh air on such a beautiful day will help to keep the grim events of the past that I'm about to relate in perspective."

19

BACK IN TIME

B rother Benedikt went back to the bar to let the other staff know he'd be away for a while. Then he showed the women outside again. Once they had passed St Margaret's church, he pointed out the white St Adalbert pavilion, built in the proximity of a spring and an ancient water mill. Then, as if by Prague magic, they were in the thick of a forest, Leon finding a little path between the trees engrossing to say the least. As for Etta and Dora, before they had time to realise it, they were again travelling back through the years to Prague's past.

"It was in 1950 when the Soviets rounded up all the priests and monks, taking them from the churches and monasteries and sending them to work in labour camps, where isolation and hard conditions waited for them. I was just a youngster, but I can still remember the horror on my parents' faces as we witnessed the scene, the Monastery being emptied of those nice chanting monks. It was then that I decided I'd become a monk myself.

"Ten years later, I did just that, but I didn't enjoy the peaceful life for long. In 1960, I was condemned to 12 years in concentration camps. I started work in the Jáchymov uranium mines. Barely fed, we had to carry enormous weights all day long, and we were given no protection from radiation when handling our loads with our bare hands.

"The mines closed in 1964, and then I was sent to work in the Soviet chemical factories. The work was much lighter, but again, we were given nothing to protect ourselves from contact with toxic material."

"How terrible!" Dora cried.

"True, but during those years in the uranium mines, I met Father Josef Zvěřina, a man of great faith who taught me that the only way not to succumb to fear, isolation, punishment and hunger is to rise above yourself and your pain, to think of yourself as part of a collective striving for their rights.

"It was the best lesson I've ever learnt in my entire life, not to be a prisoner of fear. So when my sentence was shortened in 1968 because of the events of the Prague Spring, I knew exactly what I had to do. Even when the Soviets put an end to that period of hope, I had learned to hope beyond all the odds, and to make that hope more real, I had to take action. There followed years of imprisonment, interspersed with intervals of freedom."

Once again, a person from Prague had mentioned the Prague Spring, and once again, both Etta and Dora felt the cruelty of that hope being snatched away. The Czechoslovak people had thought they had finally found their way to freedom, only to be subdued by another equally cruel dictatorship.

From the thick of the forest, they came upon a beautiful wrought-iron gate in a brick wall running parallel to their path. From a large group of keys tinkling around his waist, the monk selected one and opened the gate, letting Dora and Etta inside a graveyard shadowed by tall trees. On their right, a red roof undulated over two round windows in a peculiar little building; it would have looked like architecture more suited to hobbits than humans were it not for the Gothic tower on the side.

"That is the St Lazarus Chapel," the monk said, leading the way between simple tombs resting beside monumental ones. Dora appreciated the statues of angels crying for the departure of loved ones. He took them to where the vegetation was thicker and the path less trodden, clearing the way by moving branches aside, then showed them a little tombstone with a picture of a young man and the date 1985.

The two women didn't need to ask. The family resemblance spoke for itself.

"Eva Kladivova's brother!"

"That's right," the monk confirmed. "He was killed by the secret police. Someone betrayed him. He was one of the first signatories of Charter 77 – it seemed like a revolutionary thing, but really we were just demanding respect for our human rights. His sister was arrested, too, but Eva had never been involved in his activities, and after a few weeks, she was released. At that time, I was enjoying a spell out of prison, but it wasn't easy to get his body back for burial. We had to ask a politician whose wife we knew to be a secret Catholic to intercede."

"How did the man die?"

"He was killed during an interrogation by the STB. Eva saw him being tortured to death."

"That is so awful…"

"The times were awful then. This is why you see me here – I'm still active in the congregation as I want to stay close to the younger generation because they have not seen the horrors. They have not lived in fear of a power that knows no restraints, so I want to teach them not to take democracy for granted. True, at times it might seem chaotic, not the most efficient way to do things, but we can sacrifice some efficiency in the name of freedom…"

They stood in silence for a while. Then Brother Benedikt led the two women and one dog back to the main path. Once in the warmth of the sun, they continued their conversation.

"You mentioned Mrs Temple Black. She arrived in Prague in 1989 and was soon meeting intellectuals, students, signatories of Charter 77. I believe she actively warned Washington not to give in to the Czech president's requests for the US to grant economic advantages to his country until he guaranteed he would respect his people's human rights."

"Was Ms Kladivova involved in any of this?"

"Not directly, but I know she helped out. But she warned her staff – the ones sympathetic to the rebels – to be careful, not to trust their colleagues. She would pretend to hold them back after hours to do extra work so they could stay and photocopy their material when the others weren't about."

"But why would someone kill Eva Kladivova now for allowing someone to make photocopies in her office almost three decades ago? How about the Embassy? Was there any betrayal there?"

"Ambassador Temple Black knew exactly how things worked, that anyone she trusted could be an informant, if that is what you're thinking. In fact, when the protest demonstrations started at the end of the summer of 1989, she wanted to go out and see for herself how the dissidents were being treated. But the Government encouraged all Embassy personnel to stay put and not to join these illegal demonstrations as the police had the right to intervene. Mrs Black knew that if she did as the Government asked, there would be no international witnesses, thus allowing the police to be as violent as they wanted. She told her staff to stay away, then guess where she and her husband went."

"To join the protest?"

"Exactly. That way, she didn't compromise US Diplomacy as she had given the correct orders to her staff, and informants could confirm that. But she was sure she'd be followed by the informers, and that the Czech authorities would know she was where the action was taking place, so if violence occurred, she'd be there to witness it. It was a risk, but she had a clear vision of what she had to do. This was why she was so passionate about meeting intellectuals – people who were not steeped in bureaucracy and could tell her how real Czech citizens were reacting. That was the only way to be prepared."

"Did she ever mention people she didn't trust among her staff or attending these meetings?"

"Yes, she said she was sure there were informants, maybe amongst her Czech staff or the people she was inviting in to meet with. Someone was passing information to the secret police as some of what had been said in private conversations became known by the authorities. But no one knew who it was."

"This is interesting, although I still wonder if it can have anything to do with Ms Kladivova's death. But we have no other lead at the moment. By the way, we are going to meet Christine Coleman on Monday, but she's not been at the Embassy long enough to know anything from that far back…"

"Not directly, no," said Brother Benedikt. "But in her position, she will surely have access to the cables."

"The what?"

"The cables that Mrs Temple Black sent back to Washington daily. Telephone calls could be intercepted, but these confidential cables contained detailed reports of what was going on. You might find something interesting there."

～

"Do we really only have one lead?" asked Dora as they were making their way back home.

"I don't know. It all seems so complicated and we don't have access to enough people to find out more. The police have closed in on themselves and we don't have as many friends here as we did in Ærøskøbing and Rothenburg." Etta was referring back to a couple of cases they'd solved while on previous home swaps. Then, it had been enough to listen to other people's chatter to paint a picture of what was going on and uncover the motives behind the murders.

"Do you really believe looking at those cables from 1989 will help us to understand what's going on today?"

"It sounds improbable, I know, but as I said, we don't have

any other leads. We know all the people involved – Marketa, Mr Janda, Mr Zima, Mr Smolak – were connected to the US Embassy at the time of the Velvet Revolution."

"But not Eva Kladivova so much, although Marketa mentioned Mrs Black meeting her, too. Yes, at that time, all things centred around the US Embassy. Then in the aftermath of the Velvet Revolution, they scattered far and wide. But a week ago, by chance, they were all drawn together again. Do you think Eva's murderer has killed Marketa, too?"

"I'm afraid so. She was working at the Embassy back in 1989 and she had the complete confidence and trust of Mrs Temple Black. Maybe she was in a position to provide us with some evidence to identify the murderer, or maybe she even knew who he or she is."

"But she didn't mention anything when we visited…"

"Maybe she hadn't put all the pieces of the jigsaw together, but the murderer knew she could become their Achilles' heel."

"Do you think he or she has already disposed of Marketa's body?"

"Likely, and on this occasion, he or she would have had more time and a better knowledge of where to tip her into the Vltava so the river would not return her so soon."

Head down, eyes on the ground, Etta looked like the hound when he was captured by a scent, ignoring everything around her. Even the incongruous pair of rhinos' heads on one of Břevnov's main doors.

20

VILLA PETSCHEK

On Monday at midday, Etta, Dora and Leon were waiting in Tržiště Street. Once the security checks were over, they were admitted to Villa Petschek, also known as the Schönborn Palace and the site of the US Embassy since 1945. Christine came over to welcome them, apologising for having to keep them waiting while she attended an unforeseen meeting and saying she had arranged a guided tour for them so they could see the building, and she'd meet up with them again in 45 minutes. Dora was more than enthusiastic – what an honour to visit the US Embassy! The oak-panelled library, the luxury of the gold room, the refined elegance of the music room, but mostly it was the winter garden and its piece of mechanical art that allowed the entire wall of three richly decorated arched doors to slide down and disappear below ground, opening up the view beyond the pair of marble columns to the beautiful park outside that drove Dora into transports of delight.

Their young guide was proud to show them everything. "It's a real treasure for both us Americans and the Czech people," he would repeat in response to every expression of wonder from the women. As for Leon, he was happy to explore the park and the Gloriette: the cream-coloured pavilion flying the US flag in the middle of a garden so large, he couldn't see the other end of it. He was soon lost in dreams of perfect sunsets with Guendaline at his side, leading her safely to the shelter of the charming Gloriette when a sudden thunderstorm struck...

"It's time for me to take you back to Christine," the young man said, looking at his watch.

"Have you been here for long?" Dora asked him courteously.

"It'll be a year in a couple of months' time."

"Have you heard that Mrs Shirley Temple Black was once US Ambassador?"

"Sure, during the Velvet Revolution. We still have a few photos of her time here."

"Really?"

"Yes, I'm sure Mrs Coleman will be only too happy to show you the old albums."

The man knocked on one of the creamy arched doors and Christine welcomed them in to take a seat on a sofa close to a marble fireplace.

"Would you like some coffee or tea?"

"Tea please," said Dora.

"Coffee for me," said Etta.

"And how about this charming dog?"

"I think he's had more than enough food for the day," said Etta.

Leon would have been mad at her, were it not for the fact that his mind, body and even stomach were temporarily filled with visions of a splendid she-Basset. He sighed and crashed onto the floor.

After the drinks had arrived accompanied by a few small sandwiches, after Dora had commented on the beauty of the palace and deliciousness of the food, Etta grew tired of all the pleasantries.

"We cannot find Marketa!" The words burst out of her.

"What do you mean, you cannot find her? Don't you have her phone number?"

Dora patiently explained everything that had happened, from their visit to Marketa to the discovery that she was not in Karlštejn after all.

"My goodness, this sounds rather strange. I'm sure you've told the police."

"That's another issue," said Etta, rolling her eyes. "When we spoke to Lieutenant Baloun after the attack on us, he didn't seem particularly concerned, and it was even worse when we told him about Marketa not replying to our messages. On Saturday, Marketa's cousin, Anne, came to Prague to report her cousin missing. Her statement was filed, and the police even accompanied her to Marketa's place, which was found to be in perfect order, but her overall impression, she told us yesterday, was that the police didn't take her seriously enough.

"'An adult is free to leave whenever they want to go wherever they want without explanation,' they said. So no, we haven't got in touch again with Baloun, fearing we'd get the same treatment, or worse."

"Really? It's a pretty poor show if he's neglected to investigate a possible threat to your safety. But don't you worry, I'll make a couple of calls and I'm sure he will listen to you then. But I can't think what might have happened to dear Marketa. How is it possible that she's missing? Why her?"

"We've been searching for something – anything – linking Marketa and Eva Kladivova," explained Dora.

"And the only thing we could come up with is that all this has something to do with the past."

"Maybe something that happened when Mrs Temple Black was the US Ambassador."

"But that was during the Velvet Revolution," said Christine in astonishment, "more than 25 years ago."

"That's the only time when Marketa's path might have crossed Ms Kladivova's significantly."

"I do have some photo albums of life at the Embassy around

the time of the Velvet Revolution. Would you like to have a look?"

"Indeed."

Christine asked her secretary to fetch the albums. The woman returned shortly.

"This one became the property of the Embassy after Mrs Temple Black died," Christine said, picking one out from the pile of albums. "We have copies of some of these photos, but this album is as good as a personal journal of Mrs Temple Black's time here."

Etta and Dora browsed through the photos. Shame on them, but they could only recognise the famous actress; none of the important characters who had shaped the recent history of the Czech Republic were familiar to them. Luckily, Christine was there to tell them who Václav Havel was, who Alexander Dubček was and point out the other dissidents during the Communist times.

"This is the same picture we saw at Marketa's!" said Dora, recognising the photo that included Mr Janda and Mr Zima.

"That was a very special moment," replied Christine, nodding. "It was taken in November 1989 when it became clear the Czechoslovak people were on their way to achieving democracy. We have an enlarged copy of this very picture hanging on the wall in the library."

"Have you?"

Christine took them to the library they had visited earlier on, when they hadn't noticed the photograph as it was partly concealed in a niche between two oak bookcases.

"But this one has Mr Smolak in it, too," said Dora, peering closely at the photo. It was slightly different to the one they had seen in the album.

"Of course, he was part of the staff during the Velvet Revolution. All these people made a valuable contribution to the peace that followed."

"Maybe not all," whispered Etta.

"Why do you say that?"

"Someone we spoke to mentioned the fact that information made its way out of the Embassy, that there could have been a traitor."

"Really? If that was the case, I see what you mean. I guess there must have been a traitor among them, and I'm sure Mrs Black was aware of that, too. Isn't it sad – you never know who you can trust."

"You've no idea who that person could be?"

Christine's eyes moved from one face to the other on the picture. They all seemed so proud of what they had done.

"No, I don't, and it'd be very unfair of me to speculate about any of them. They all put their lives at risk and it could have been anyone. It could have been a cleaner or maintenance person, working odd hours and placing hidden bugs for the STB."

"Brother Benedikt mentioned a series of cables that Mrs Black sent almost daily to Washington."

"Yes, every Ambassador has to report their work and findings."

"We were wondering if we could have a look at those?"

"The cables?"

"Yes. You still have them, don't you?"

"Of course, but it's official documentation. It's not been made public yet."

"But it was such a long time ago…"

"I know, but these documents can only be shared with the public after they have been declassified."

"No exception?"

"Well, I'd need to ask for authorisation, and that in itself would be a lengthy process."

"What if you were to go through them yourself and see if there's anything that sheds light on the present case or the relationships between the people involved?"

"People involved with whom?"

"Marketa, or Ms Kladivova. Or maybe you'll uncover people mentioned in those documents who were also present the night of the concert."

"There won't have been many there who would be old enough. Most of the people networking after the concert were young entrepreneurs."

"But something might jump out at you."

"OK, I will ask my secretary to search our archives for the relevant cables and I will read through them. If I find anything of interest, I may be able to arrange special dispensation for the police..."

"Will it be difficult to find those documents?"

"No, they're all filed, and in my role, I am allowed access to them."

"That's awesome."

"In the meantime," said Christine, "I'll call the Police Chief and ask him for an update, and why the assault on my friends has not been given due consideration. And I'll ask him if he knows that Marketa Ciprova, another person present at the concert the night Ms Kladivova died, seems to have disappeared into thin air..."

∾

THAT EVENING, ETTA RECEIVED A CALL. "HELLO, MRS PAA-SS-O-liii-nna... can't I just call you Mrs Fletcher? It's difficult enough for the average Czech policeman to speak in English, but if I have to drop in some Italian, I'm afraid this is asking too much."

"Lieutenant Baloun?" said Etta, recognising his voice.

"Yes, that's me. I've been called by Chief Pommer. He's not happy that I didn't give you my undivided attention, and now I'm obliged to make up for it. That is, if you intend to collaborate with me and save me from losing all my stripes and going back to being a simple cop..."

"Is this an official call?"

"I suppose it is, except for the introduction."

"And what comes after the introduction?"

"An official request for you to join me at Marketa Ciprova's house in Nový Svět tomorrow morning. Would 10am be OK or will that interrupt your sleuthing in another part of town?"

"Ten in the morning will be fine. Have you finally decided to enter her home and see what's going on? Do you want us to tell you if we spot anything that seems different to a week ago?"

"Something like that. In fact, we were there on Saturday with Marketa's cousin from Karlštejn. Not that she noticed anything unusual. And we were there again today, all afternoon. I believe the scene of crime officers have pretty much finished their job, and now I'm allowed to invite people round."

So, the police think a crime has been committed, then? Etta thought. "OK, see you tomorrow, then," she said, putting down the phone. "Well," she commented, explaining the conversation to Dora, "it seems Christine's call changed Baloun's mind immediately. On the other hand, the Lieutenant said that forensics have been in Marketa's house all afternoon, so that can't be because of Christine's phone call to the Police Chief, as they would already have been there by then. Maybe they didn't dismiss Anne's statement as useless after all."

"Maybe he is just doing his job," said Dora shyly, feeling guilty that the Lieutenant had been reproached by his superiors, but at the same time not wanting to provoke Etta.

"Miss Dorotea Rosa Pepe, don't you dare sympathise with that man!" Etta said.

Dora sighed. As usual, Etta had seen right through her.

21

THE MISSING PHOTOGRAPH

The next morning, Leon woke his two bipeds up rather early. When he had looked from the window, he'd found himself eye to eye with Guendaline. They had stood there, looking at each other for a moment that seemed as long as an eternity and as sweet as a huge strawberry and whipped-cream sponge cake. Then Guendaline was called away from the window and Leon wondered if she was going out. He had no hesitation in harassing the two women out of their beds and into their clothes until they were ready to go out, too.

It was seven o'clock as he pulled the two of them towards Petřín park; he'd sniffed Guendaline going the same way. Despite Etta alternately squawking, grumbling and gawking, Leon kept dragging with all his might until he came across his beloved and her human.

Leon stood petrified, his legs shaking with emotion. He didn't dare take a single step in case he collapsed, having forgotten which of his four legs he needed to move first and what the right sequence would be from there.

"I knew a woman had to be the cause of all this fuss," said Etta, watching the other Basset.

"She's such a cutie pie, no wonder our Leon is in love," whispered Dora.

In love? Is that it? wondered the poor hound, who had feared he had caught some terrible disease.

Guendaline came over to him, sniffing him here and there while Leon stood still as a statue, forgetting all about dog etiquette. And when he was on the point of swooning, the lovely she-Basset stretched her front legs, her bum up in the air, an unmistakable invitation to play.

It took a long moment before Leon could unfreeze. Guendaline jumped around him, again inviting him to play, then barking in protest at his lack of reaction. Meanwhile, her human had joined Etta and Dora, greeting them in Czech then, realising her mistake, resorting to English.

"You can unleash your dog if you want. In this park, they don't mind if dogs are allowed to run free, provided they don't attack anyone."

"I don't think Leon will be interested in attacking anything – person, squirrel, hare – as long as Guendaline's around…"

"How do you know my dog?"

Dora explained how the two of them had met previously.

"So this is Leon! Yes, I remember him, but he was with another lady."

"That was our friend, Marketa, she took Leon for a walk while Etta and I visited the Strahov Monastery," and then Dora fell silent, once again deeply concerned for the safety of the friendly nurse.

Detached from his leash, Leon waddled around as if testing his legs for the first time. He stumbled twice, then played hide and catch and all sorts of games with Guendaline, letting her win every time. A few passers-by stopped to watch the two dogs running after each other in their green corner of the park, surrounded by clouds of lilacs. Total bliss.

Alas, all things must pass, and the woman called to Guendaline. "I'm afraid we need to go, young lady," she said, then addressing Etta and Dora, she explained, "I'm due at the office by 9am."

"Will Guendaline be all alone until you finish work?"

"No, my daughter will be back by lunchtime to let her out and keep her company, then at 5pm, my husband takes her on a longer walk before dinner. We try to make sure she's not alone for too long, and with all the exercise she's had this morning, she'll be happy to have a long nap after breakfast."

Dora looked at Leon's dreamy expression. "I'm not sure our boy will eat much today…"

They were making their way back together, chatting animatedly, when a car nearly ran them over, speeding forward without giving way to them on a pedestrian crossing. And Dora and Etta recognised the driver.

"That's Marketa's neighbour," they said in unison.

"That's also my unpopular colleague. He's been off work, pretending to be sick while he's actually driving round and round the city. To think that many young people would be glad to have his job and would work with enthusiasm. I don't know how this country of mine is going to succeed with such unproductive citizens."

"We call them wage scroungers," said Etta, acknowledging that the laziest specimens of the species existed in Italy, too.

~

AFTER A LARGE BREAKFAST THAT LEON DIDN'T EVEN SNIFF, THE TWO women walked all the way to Nový Svět. Once outside Marketa's home, which had been cordoned off by the police, Etta called the Lieutenant.

"There you are!" he said, opening the door. "The scene of crime officers have finished, but they'd still prefer us to wear shoe coverings and gloves. The dog, I'm afraid, won't be allowed in; I don't have covers for his paws, and forensics would love the excuse to say they couldn't do their job properly as a stupid policeman allowed a dog inside."

"Then we'll have to take it in turns to go in," said Dora.

"That will never do! All great detectives need their sidekicks. What would Sherlock Holmes be without Watson, Poirot without Hastings, Nero Wolfe without Archie Goodwin...?"

"So what do you suggest?" Etta cut off what was threatening to grow into a long list.

"Follow me." The man walked the few metres separating them from the café where they had gone to enquire about Marketa a few days earlier. "Dear lady, may I wish you a very good morning and a successful day..."

"What do you want?" the café owner answered dryly, but her bright pink lips opened in a smile.

"This humble servant of yours wondered if you could take care of this dog while I show these two ladies the crime scene..."

"They aren't suspects, are they?"

"Of course not, they're our Italian collaborators, our secret weapon sent to help the useless Prague police."

The woman laughed and moved closer to Leon, shaking hands with the three humans. "I know these three. This cute boy might enjoy a little breakfast while he's waiting."

"I'm not sure he will eat," said Dora.

"Separation anxiety?"

"Kind of, but not from us. He's in love with the neighbour's Basset Hound. She is a cutie, I must say."

"Leon, my son!" The Lieutenant was wearing an aggrieved expression. "Trust your bacon more than your women."

The café owner scratched Leon under his ears. So melancholy was his expression, she couldn't help landing a smacking kiss on his head, which left a formidable pink tattoo in his fur. Leon wondered why the Almighty had made him so irresistible to humans, when all he wanted was Guendaline's love. He sighed and crashed to the ground, only to raise his head a second later as the bacon hit the pan. Maybe the Lieutenant was right after all.

~

WHEN THEY RETURNED TO MARKETA'S BUILDING, THE NASTY neighbour was unloading a large number of supermarket bags from his car into his secret garden. He stopped to look at them, but when Etta glared at him, he disappeared inside.

The Lieutenant handed the women some latex gloves, saying, "Although it's better if you don't touch anything yet." When they had all put on shoe coverings, he finally opened Marketa's door, inviting the two women in. Despite what Anne had told them, they had half expected to find the house all messed up with signs of a struggle evident, but everything was in its proper place in the living room. The bed was made in the bedroom, but in the kitchen sink was a mug and a dish, and a strange smell lingered in the air.

It was Dora who opened the cupboard under the sink to reveal an empty rubbish bin.

"The forensics took the bin bag away for analysis. You never know what you might find amongst the rubbish."

"But what about the fact there was a full rubbish bag?" said Etta.

The Lieutenant looked at her quizzically.

"If she knew she was going away, she would have disposed of it," Dora explained. "Marketa was –is – a model of efficiency, so she wouldn't have left anything in the sink, either, not even a mug. The rest of the house is spotlessly clean, as it was when we visited."

"Hmmm," mumbled the Lieutenant. It was hard to say if he was impressed with their reasoning or about to discard it entirely.

They moved back into the living room, where Dora noticed something else. "The Embassy photograph is gone!" she said, pointing to the little table where a number of portraits were carefully displayed.

"What photograph?" asked Etta, lost in the forest of images.

"The one of Marketa and Mrs Temple Black, Mr Zima and Mr Janda and the other staff, like the one that we saw at the Embassy."

"You are right, it's not here."

They looked around. On the other pieces of furniture, more framed pictures were displayed. Had it been moved somewhere else? No, it wasn't there at all.

"Maybe you'd like to share with this poor policeman of yours what's missing?"

"I'm not sure if it's important or not," said Dora, telling him about the photo.

"So Zima and Janda were in that portrait?" he asked for confirmation.

"And other Embassy staff from 1989."

"Are you sure the picture was there?"

"Absolutely."

The Lieutenant suggested they have another look in the bedroom. Maybe Marketa's interest had been piqued by their conversation the previous week and she had taken the photograph to bed with her to examine it before going to sleep. It wasn't there. Dora explained it was in a silver frame about the size of a sheet of A4 – not small enough to go unseen.

"So that's about the only thing we know she took with her," said the Lieutenant. "I want you to describe that picture to me as well as you can."

"We can do better than that, I can show you a copy," said Etta, taking out her mobile.

"You took a shot? So marvellously intuitive of you."

"No, I didn't, but we saw a copy of that picture at the Embassy. I'm asking Christine if she can send us a photo of it straight away."

It only took a few seconds for Christine to reply that she was out of the office, but she had asked a member of staff to take a shot. An instant later, a photo had landed in Etta's inbox and the Lieutenant was examining it.

"There's Mr Smolak, too," he said.

"Yes, Christine said that they probably took it in turns to take the photos. In the picture Marketa had, Mr Smolak wasn't there."

"This is no good," he muttered. "I wonder if there are other differences in the picture Marketa had compared to this one. There might be other people missing."

"At the Embassy, they have the exact copy of Marketa's picture in Mrs Temple Black's album. They have sent the wrong one. Perhaps you could ask the Embassy to lend you the album?"

"It's not easy negotiating with an Embassy," Baloun was thinking aloud. "But I'm a mere man, I can only deal with one problem at a time. Let's focus on why the photo would have disappeared in the first place."

"It shouldn't be too difficult to work that out. Maybe whoever caused Marketa to disappear didn't want us to examine the picture too closely. They didn't want us to know they've got any link with Marketa and this history."

"But that rules Mr Janda out. He was quite happy to arrange to meet up with her when we were all together at the theatre," said Dora.

"That was before anything happened. Maybe he didn't know then that events were going to present him with an ideal opportunity to kill Eva Kladivova. Or maybe it was Mr Zima who attacked Marketa and wanted the picture to disappear."

"Or maybe it was someone else in the group who we don't recognise."

"Maybe another person who was at the concert."

"Or maybe we missed a detail in the photo we should have noticed ..."

"Do you mind if I say something?" the Lieutenant asked as if he was the least important person in the room.

"Go ahead," said Dora.

"If you really have to," added Etta.

"Thank you both. I think I might need your skills in setting up international relationships."

The women looked at him without understanding.

"You see, Embassy officials are not very cooperative towards a poor police officer. They will close up like a hedgehog and refuse to disclose any information, or they'll take such a long time to reveal it, I'll be retired before I get what I need..."

"You want us to ask Christine for the exact picture we saw here at Marketa's?" said Etta.

"And possibly with a full list of names of the people who appear in the picture. Tell her we have no reason to think any American is involved, but we need names of all the Czechs. And stress that this is a trail that probably won't lead us anywhere, but we need to eliminate it from our enquiries."

"Why do you think it won't lead us anywhere?"

"Because it happened almost 30 years ago."

"Yet someone felt compelled to remove that photograph."

"Or it was Marketa who took it away with her for sentimental reasons."

"Marketa has been kidnapped, and most likely killed! We too were attacked, and if it weren't for Mr Smolak helping us out..."

"Tut, tut," said the Lieutenant, lowering his eyes. "I know." But the wry expression on his face screamed that he didn't care much.

They went to fetch Leon, who was looking at the café counter in the not-so-secret hope that a second round of breakfast would soon be served, thoughts of Guendaline put aside for the moment. Among the continuous stream of people coming and going, most reached out to pet him or asked the café owner why this poor doggy had been left to starve. As it turned out, his bipeds, too, found the smells coming from the kitchen enticing, so they decided to stay for a pastry and a cup of coffee, while the

Lieutenant reluctantly acknowledged that he had to go and wouldn't be able to join them.

~

"WHAT DID YOU MAKE OF THAT?" ETTA ASKED AFTER BALOUN HAD departed.

"I believe that picture will put the police on the tracks of the killer. Don't you think?"

"I don't know. Behind all his teasing and jokes, the Lieutenant seems determined to ignore facts such as us being attacked. And why has he called this look at the past pointless?"

"Maybe he thinks we have simply had our heads turned by all the fascinating stories we've heard about the Velvet Revolution."

"But every lead we've followed has taken us into the past. I'm more convinced than ever we need to examine that first."

"Well in that case, it's good he's asked us to get a copy of the picture."

"Indeed, but let's not tell Christine it's a request from the police."

"But it'll be unfair to lie to her, after she's been so kind to us."

"I know, but I'm really afraid she might refuse…"

"And while I think about it, why didn't you tell the Lieutenant about our meeting with Brother Benedikt, or the cables?"

"We don't yet know if we're going to find anything of interest in the cables. Also, I have a strange feeling that it might not be wise to tell him everything about our sleuthing. He seems far too nice to our faces, then he doesn't take action when we'd expect him to. At times, I wonder…" and Etta left the sentence to linger unfinished in the air.

22

THE CAMERA NEVER LIES

I t was a rainy afternoon. Etta and Dora were sitting once again on the light blue sofa in Christine's office at the Embassy, Leon at their feet. She had invited them over for a cup of hot tea served in delicate porcelain cups, accompanied by tasty American cookies. Christine also had some biscuits she'd baked for her own dog, and that attention to detail, along with the warm, thick carpet on the floor, upgraded the Embassy to a five-star hotel in the hound's eyes. A pity the women were sitting around, talking nonsense, but a hard-working Basset could always enjoy a good nap.

"I'm afraid it will take some time before the cables that Shirley Temple Black sent back to Washington are declassified. The procedure has only just started."

"Was it started automatically or upon request?" Etta asked.

"That's an astute question. Apparently, another former US Ambassador to Prague wants to write the story of the events surrounding the Velvet Revolution, so he made the request for declassification as he needs some of the material in the cables. It will take time, I guess…"

"But if the former Ambassador wants to publish details from

the cables in the near future, he must have examined them and believe there's nothing compromising in them."

Christine shrugged, pointing to two large folders on her desk. "I can tell you this: I went through those cables myself and found them compelling. I also feel sure there's nothing compromising in them, nor anything connected to Eva's sad death, but until the process of declassification is over, I can't allow you to read them. I'm sure you understand…"

"But there's been a murder! We're only asking to hurry up a process that's already started."

Christine shook her head. "Embassies have strict rules to adhere to." As she looked again at the volumes on her desk, she was interrupted by an incoming call. "That'll be my secretary, reminding me it's time to join a meeting in the next room. But you can stay here and wait for me if you wish."

"Oh no, I think we'd better go ho… ouch!" Dora cried out as Etta kicked her in the shin with all her might.

"That's a kind offer, Christine." Etta's face broke into an innocent smile. "It will give us a little time to recover after what's been a rather long day."

"Then I'll ask my secretary to bring you another pot of tea."

"That would be highly appreciated." As Christine finally answered the phone, Etta tilted her head as she'd seen Leon doing when he was conquering people's hearts.

As soon as Christine left, Dora looked at her friend for an explanation as to why she had been kicked so violently.

"She's left the cables," Etta whispered, nodding to the folders on the desk.

"Mrs Concetta Natale Passolina, you don't want to take a look at them after what Christine told us, do you?"

"Miss Dorotea Rosa Pepe, why do you think she left us, and them, in here?"

"Because you mentioned we were tired…" then lightning struck. "You mean she did it on purpose so that…"

"Exactly. Rules are rules. She can't give us express permission to read them, but one day, those documents will be declassified anyway. She's looked at them, the former Ambassador has gone through them. They're just history, although I do hope they can provide us with important clues."

Once the secretary had delivered the promised pot of fresh tea, Etta opened up the first folder. The cables were in official language, but she soon felt in tune with the person who'd written them. It was easy to perceive Mrs Temple Black's impressions, her determination to get through those harsh times and avoid a repeat of what she'd witnessed back in 1968.

As Christine had said, the cables were as enthralling as a good spy story. When the light outside started to dim, Etta realised that it'd take much longer than she'd anticipated to go through them all.

"The only solution is to take pictures," she suggested.

"And then I can pull them from my phone on to the tablet for ease of reading. I should also be able to compile them into pdf documents ..."

Etta looked at Dora as if she was speaking Chinese. Dora explained that going through the images one at a time would be tiring, but pdf documents would allow them to display them one after the other like the pages of a book. Etta still didn't understand much, but she conceded that Dora was much better than her at computer stuff. She simply volunteered to turn and flatten the pages whilst Dora took the pictures.

This long and boring job was interrupted by a sudden knock at the door. The women's hearts sank in horror; they only just had time to close all the folders and pretend to be sitting quietly and chatting when Christine's secretary brought in more tea and cookies, the friendly smile on her face eliciting looks of pure wide-eyed innocence from the two guests.

As soon as the secretary was gone, Etta and Dora resumed their frenzied activity. Then they looked through the photo album that Christine had so very thoughtfully left lying around, studying every single face. Each picture had a caption, naming the people from left to right by row.

"Do you recognise anyone else?"

"I confess, I was wondering if that isn't our very own Lieutenant Baloun," replied Etta, pointing to one of the pictures. "But I can't find his name in the caption. Then again, he wouldn't have asked for a copy of the photo if he thought we might spot him."

Dora sighed and kept taking pictures as Etta continued. "The Lieutenant will get the photos from the album and the list of names, but let's not tell him about the cables yet."

～

AFTER A WHOLE DAY OF RAIN, A LIGHT FOG HAD ENVELOPED THE streets of Prague. The cast-iron lamps were on and the bells of St Nicholas's were chiming over a deserted Malostranské náměstí.

As Etta, Dora and Leon were crossing the square, a slender shadow in a trench coat approached them. The fur on the back of Leon's neck bristled, Dora opened her mouth in shock, Etta's eyebrows shot up. She started to swing her tote bag, ready to hit out hard if necessary, for once grateful that no matter how much she emptied her bag, it was always far too heavy.

"Have you got what I need with you?" a voice whispered, the huge sunglasses covering the eyes underneath the figure's hat totally unnecessary after dark on an already dull day.

"But it's you, Lieutenant," Dora cried, recognising the man under the stereotypical private eye disguise.

Baloun removed his glasses, pushing back his Fedora hat. "I thought I might have fooled you."

Leon wagged his tail in recognition and the man high-fived him before scratching his head.

"What are you doing with these two, boy? At this hour, you should be enjoying the night with some sassy lady Basset…"

"Please, don't put ideas in his head."

"Have you got my stuff?" he asked, again adopting the husky, mysterious voice.

"Oh please, stop pretending we're collaborators..."

"But that is exactly what we are."

Etta shrugged. The man was an incorrigible joker.

"I don't know how your colleagues put up with you."

"Oh, I cause them a great deal of trouble."

"How have you lasted this long in the police force, then?"

"That's what my boss asks me every time he sees me."

"You're not that bad," said Dora. For the life of her, she couldn't understand why someone would insult another human being in the name of humour.

"Anyway," Etta cut her short, "to answer your question, we've done our bit."

The man stretched out his hand as if to receive what was due to him, causing Etta to shrink back, both her hands protectively around her tote bag.

"I'll give you the photos," she said, "and the list of names, but only if you let me have a list of all the guests who were present at the concert."

"But that's private."

"As is this stuff from the Embassy."

"You drive such a hard bargain."

"Yes, I'm from the South."

"It wasn't meant as a compliment."

"I don't care."

"OK, I'll give you the list, but if anyone asks, it's not come from me, otherwise the Embassy might ask for my head and my boss will be only too happy to oblige. We never had this conversation, OK?"

"What conversation?" Etta winked at him.

The Lieutenant pointed to an old car in an awful aubergine colour, double parked on the side of the square. He went over to it, took some crumpled papers from the back and returned to the women. The documents were exchanged, Etta sending him the photo file via her mobile.

"I take it as given that if you come up with anything useful, you will give me a call. Won't you?"

"Of course," said Etta, her face deadpan. "And you'll do the same?"

"You can't ask me to do that, I'm in the police. Much as I'd love to cooperate with Mrs Fletcher, there are things that even a crooked policeman like me cannot do."

"You know best," said Etta, turning her head dismissively.

"But you're an ally of the good guys... aren't you?"

"I'll think about it, but I don't really believe in unbalanced relationships."

~

AFTER DINNER, ETTA AND DORA DECIDED THEY'D START ON THE pictures. It was an easier job than tackling the cables and they did not want to hand an advantage to the Lieutenant. They went through the two lists of people, but the only names common to both the Korean concert and the old Embassy pictures were Marketa Ciprova, Josef Janda, Michal Smolak and Egon Zima.

"Could someone be using an alias?" asked Etta, annoyed.

"Or simply have married and changed their name?" Dora suggested.

"That's a good observation. If it's just about changing surname, we could look for women's first names that appear on both lists, and then ask the police to find out if those people are married and registered for their concert ticket using their husbands' surnames."

Of the six women in the pictures, only one bore the same first name as a woman on the theatre list. But in the Embassy photo, she already looked to be in her fifties, so assuming it was the same person, she must now be over 75. Would a woman of that age be able to attack Eva Kladivova, and then kidnap and maybe kill Marketa?

"It doesn't make sense," said Etta, discomfited.

"Shall we move on to the cables?"

"Why not? Hopefully, we will find something more interesting there."

It wasn't long before they realised some of the cables were missing. Perhaps the folder they had been looking at only contained the ones that would be declassified as they didn't contain sensitive information. Evidently, even after 30 years, some things still needed to be kept secret.

Etta looked discouraged. "Let's just hope what we're looking for isn't in the missing cables," said Dora.

It was past 10pm when they spotted the names Josef Janda and Egon Zima. Both were described as honest men who had not yet realised what it was like to operate in a free market.

"I wonder," commented Mrs Temple Black, "how we can best help them with the transition."

They read about a few meetings between Mrs Temple Black and Brother Benedikt, how he had helped the Ambassador, along with a series of intellectuals, to understand what the Communist regime had been like, the role of fear and suspicion in controlling people. Mr Smolak was referred to as a good local resource, an efficient and clever man who knew his way around public offices.

Marketa popped up here and there. "She's an industrious woman, our Marketa Ciprova, and I'm sure I can trust her," Mrs Temple Black had written, going on to say what a relief it was for the embassy staff to know they had someone prepared, available and trustworthy should they need help. But in a more confidential cable, Mrs Temple Black declared, "There must be someone here at the Embassy who's passing on information. When I met President Husák, he knew things he could not have known unless he had an informant here at the Embassy, either full time or visiting regularly. I wonder if I can set a trap to find out who it is..."

Annoyingly, there was no follow-up to this. If the Ambassador had set her trap and caught her traitor, there was no record of it.

~

IT WAS MIDNIGHT WHEN ETTA AND DORA DECIDED TO CALL IT A night and head for their beds. Sleep caught Etta unawares and she fell into a deep slumber until the bells struck 3am. Then she woke up with a train of thought speeding through her brain. Actually, it was more like a puffing old steam locomotive approaching slowly from afar, but still, you can't look away as it gradually gets closer.

She needed a connection between the Embassy and Eva Kladivova, between Marketa and Ms Kladivova, something strong enough to justify a murder, possibly two murders, after more than 25 years. It made no sense. Maybe, as was her habit, Etta had dug a hole for herself, searching for a secret from the past that simply wasn't there. The problem was that once she started digging, she couldn't stop, not even when she hit a wall.

It was time to put things into perspective. What if the killer was Mr Zima or Mr Janda? They each had a good motive to kill Ms Kladivova, she having been respectively a rich ex-wife and... what were the man's words? A cutthroat competitor. But why get rid of Marketa too? That had been the stumbling block all along.

Of course, the concert connected Ms Kladivova and Marketa. That night, had Marketa seen something – something she possibly wasn't aware of at the time, but the killer knew she had witnessed it? If only Ms Kladivova had been poisoned, Marketa might have seen someone interfering with her glass or food. But the woman had been stabbed. If Marketa had seen something, it must have been subtle – so subtle she hadn't mentioned it to Etta and Dora when they'd met up.

"Like what, though?" Etta growled to herself. "Concetta Natale Passolina, are you digging just for the fun of burying yourself? Enough!" She settled down in her bed and switched off the light, crashing her head against the pillow and shutting her eyes. But to her great annoyance, instead of going blank, her mind pictured a group of people. And they were not any old people; she'd seen them before.

"Marketa's photograph!" cried Etta, sitting up again. What had the killer decided was so dangerous about that stupid photograph that they had to make sure it vanished? Did they not know there were copies of it at the Embassy, too? Why take the risk that someone would notice the picture was missing, which would only draw attention to its significance? Because it was less risky than having someone look at it and realise that... that...

That what? If only she could answer this.

She breathed deeply and switched the light back on, annoying Leon so immensely, he decided to move to Dora's room in protest.

"Here's a fine example of a canine's sense of sacrifice. What kind of family dog are you?" she shouted after him, but the hound didn't even turn his head.

In a frenzy of impatience, she reached for the tablet, found the picture they had taken at the Embassy library and stared at it one more time, taking in all details of Janda and Zima. How were they dressed? Was their hair combed? Did they have anything in their hands? Was anyone else in the group eyeing them meaningfully? Not really.

Was there someone else they had been so foolish as to not recognise? She enlarged the photo, scrutinising every single face. No one sparked a flash of recognition.

"What do you do when you're solving a word search puzzle and you can no longer distinguish a single word in the forest of letters?" she asked herself. "You have to step back. Close your eyes for a few seconds, open them again and suddenly meaningful words stand out. Two seconds earlier, you couldn't see them; now it seems impossible you didn't notice them."

Doing just as she preached, Etta closed her eyes tightly, and when she opened them again, her jaw dropped in astonishment. The locomotive was now running wild, rattling loudly through her mind, each wagon carrying a vision. The tomb in the cemetery they had visited with Brother Benedikt; Eva Kladivova's expression the night of the concert; Leon pulling them back when they had left Kampa park after identifying the body; Etta herself saying the killer always returns to the crime scene. The visit to the underground parts of Prague and the guide explaining the distinction between World War Two shelters and the nuclear bunkers built during the Cold War, sometimes in private gardens. Guendaline's owner's remarks about the nasty old man who lived in Nový Svět; his large shopping bags. Finally, the last train wagon displayed a giant poster of the missing photograph – now she knew why it was so disturbing for the killer. How could she not have thought of it before when they had seen it and the other picture at the Embassy?

It seemed as if the whole train had run over her at full speed. She now knew the killer's reasonings, his whys. Sitting on the edge of her bed, her hands tightening on the duvet as if it could help her survive the blow, she took the best part of an hour to piece the whole story together. Then, incredible as it was, she had to acknowledge it answered all the questions, filling in all the gaps.

What now? Should she tell the police? Would they move fast enough? Better to tell Christine. But what could she tell her exactly? Her theory was no more than thin air – unless she found some proof…

Wait a second, what if she could find the nurse's body? That would be proof!

She jumped out of her bed and went to wake Dora and Leon.

It was still dark enough for them to pass through the city unobserved.

23

BEYOND THE WALL

The fog had become so thick in the streets, Etta, Dora and Leon all had the sense of still being asleep rather than in the real world. They passed the Loreto Monastery quickly, scared as they were of the statues that loomed out of the darkness and seemed to move in the flickering light of the lamps. They took Kapucínská Street, a windy never-ending passage between high walls, so narrow they feared someone would jump out on them from behind every corner. Even brave Leon stopped time and time again to look at them as if to make sure it was absolutely necessary to carry on.

With relief, they found themselves on Nový Svět. They passed Marketa's door and stopped a few metres further on at a gate in the wall on the opposite side where they had seen her neighbour, the man with the mean brown eyes, entering a garden. The big lock looked so robust that Etta immediately rejected the idea of getting in that way. As the two women looked around, Leon managed to squeeze beneath the gate, but he was on the leash so they had to pull him back.

"I wish I were thin," Dora said, appreciating the fact that her round bum and belly made Leon look slim.

"Leave it out!" Etta said, always touchy on the subject of weight and dieting. "We have everything we need to get in," and she pointed to a wheelie bin sitting next to the café. When they moved it along the cobbled street, the noise sounded deafening in the quiet of early morning. All the women could do was hope the residents would think it was just a couple of lost tourists dragging their cases along the road. The fog would conceal them, and maybe even muffle the sound somewhat.

Much more difficult was climbing on to the wheelie bin, which wriggled and scooted off from underneath them every time they tried. It would have actually proved impossible if it hadn't been for a bench a little further up the street. They wedged the waste bin up against it, climbed on to the bench, then on to the bin, and finally over the garden wall that – goodness! – was more than two metres high. Luckily, it was thick enough to allow them to walk along its precarious height in single file, the one in front hand in hand with the one behind to help each other balance.

Next to the gate was a sloping reinforcement behind the stone wall. That allowed them to come down safely, albeit sliding on their bums rather than standing up. Leon, who had been pushed beneath the gate, welcomed them enthusiastically, waiting for instructions on what to do next. He seemed to have forgotten his earlier fears, enjoying the thrill and the mystery of the clandestine early-morning mission.

Etta sent a beam of light from her torch all around the space beyond the wall, wondering what to do next. The garden was very large – maybe it used to be part of a public park – so it took them a while to explore its main paths, but they didn't see anything that seemed relevant. Then Dora approached Leon and whispered in his ear.

"Search!"

As most dog owners know, if you ask an untrained dog to search, they do not bother with silly questions such as, "But

ADRIANA LICIO

what should I look for exactly? A treat, a human, a woollen glove, a cat? Should I start from the left or right? Above or underground? What is the chance I will find anything interesting?" Nothing of the sort. As soon as Leon was asked to search, he simply acted. After gazing at Guendaline, searching was his second favourite activity, something that sent a primordial thrill all through his body. His fur bristling with excitement, he started by running all along the garden wall. Then he paused roughly in the mid-point of it, nose twitching, ready to catch any scent that would put him on the right track.

He rushed around in large circles, every now and then sending a furtive look Etta and Dora's way as if to ask if they'd found anything out yet. No, they hadn't; they were depending on him, so he kept trotting around on full alert.

All of a sudden, he stopped as if he had hit an invisible wall. The white tip of his tail standing rigid at a 90° angle to the rest of his quivering body, he retraced his steps. There. There was something!

His nose glued to the ground like a tram following its rails, he trotted in a precise direction. No more circling around, he was following a trail.

He went back towards the gate in the garden wall, the one he had used to get in, where a thought struck Leon: he had been following the scent the wrong way! Returning to where he had started, following exactly the same route, he kept going, only to stop abruptly next to a collection of large terracotta vases. He started to dig, his paws clawing the earth in a frenzy like those of a dog possessed. Raising his head, he let loose a deep, long howl before resuming his digging.

Etta and Dora joined him and their torchlight shone upon a concrete hatch, hidden amongst the geranium vases, half buried in the ground. A metal handle inserted into the concrete looked to be the only way to lift the hinged door and access whatever was beneath. But try as they might, the two women couldn't budge it so much as an inch. It was far too heavy.

All sweat and impatience, Etta shone the torch beam around in search of leverage of some sort.

"Stop there," murmured Dora, blocking Etta's arm and halting the beam of light. "That's a well."

"You think it might be a secondary access?" asked Etta as they moved towards it. But when she flashed the torchlight inside, the water at the bottom reflected it back at her. "Access denied!"

"I wasn't thinking of a second access; what about using the pulley that lifts the water bucket out? It may help us to lever open the hatch, if it is robust and long enough."

Etta flashed the light on the mechanism. To her surprise, the chain looked much stronger than it needed to be to lift a simple bucket of water.

"Blimey!" she cried, looking at Dora with admiration. "I think that's exactly what it's for."

Removing the bucket from the hook that also looked disproportionately large and strong, the two women unrolled the chain. It was exactly long enough to reach the hatch. They attached the hook to the handle, and seconds later, they were working the pulley. Luckily, it worked on a ratchet system, so that if they needed to pause to take a breath, the whole thing didn't roll back to its original position.

"Come on, we can do it," muttered Etta between gritted teeth.

"We're almost there," added Dora with her infinite optimism.

"Woof, woof, woof," barked the canine director of operations as he saw the door lifting on its hinges. When it reached 90°, its movement stopped. While Dora was pointing to the safety lever that would avoid the pulley rolling back, shutting them in, before either she or Etta could tell him to stop, Leon had disappeared underground.

"Thanks, Leon," Etta grumbled as the torch beam revealed the top steps of a long concrete staircase descending into a black hole. "Now, we have no choice."

"We would have gone down in any case, and we'd better be quick," Dora replied without a hint of hesitation. People-pleaser-ever-so-sweet Dora could turn into a super-heroine when required, always surprising Etta with her infinite resources. Down they crept, staying close to one another.

~

THE STAIRS SEEMED TO GO ON FOR EVER, DOWN INTO DARKNESS SO thick, the torchlight didn't reach any further than their feet. Only once they were at the bottom did their eyes get accustomed to the shadows, their gaze seeming to acquire a greater depth. Disappointingly, when Etta rotated the torchlight, all she could see were the bare walls of a large low-ceilinged room.

"Is that it?" she asked, moving around, Dora sticking to her side.

"No, there must be another room. Otherwise, where has Leon gone?"

"Let's explore." Following the wall, they stumbled behind a pillar and into a corridor. From the end of it, they heard the hound woofing, as if asking them to get a move on.

Etta stopped in her tracks. "We're walking into a trap. If the killer comes along and closes the hatch, we'll be prisoners down here and nobody will ever find us..."

"But we've come this far to see if something is wrong in here. And there's no way I'm letting you go on alone, nor going in there myself without you."

Etta sighed, admitting that was exactly how she felt.

"...and the dog must have found something..." Dora added to boost their courage.

"...and if we were to go back," Etta continued gloomily, "we'd still have nothing to say to the police. Let's go in and be done with it as soon as possible. This place is unsettling."

They came to the end of the corridor, Leon running back and

forth to speed them up. When they entered the room, the torch revealed it to be just as large as the first one they had entered, but this time, a gated iron fence separated one third of it, effectively making that part of the room into a cage. And it was there that Leon had directed his attention, his long body, like a compass needle, pointing to a corner beyond the fence.

Etta's torch revealed a simple camp bed, and on the bed, deaf to all Leon's barks, lay a body.

"Another corpse!" Etta cried, frightened.

"It can't be."

"See for yourself," said Etta stubbornly, pointing the torch to the mass of sheets and blankets.

"I see it, but I don't think it's a corpse," explained Dora. "There's no smell of decay." Which was true. The atmosphere was dreadfully heavy with the smell of damp and stale air, but that was it.

"Do you think they might still be alive, then?" asked Etta, as if there could be a third possibility.

"Yes, I think so."

They explored the iron bars of the fence and the gate set in the centre of it. Inevitably, the gate was locked. Etta pointed the torchlight around the room, pausing on a desk next to the wall. There was a lamp on it.

"Should we switch it on?" asked Dora.

"Better not, just in case someone is alerted by the sudden use of electricity down here. This must be a nuclear bunker like the one that tour guide described. But where are the keys?"

After a fruitless exploration of the desk, Dora moved on to the other piece of furniture in the room, a cupboard containing a couple of dishes and some cutlery along with various medications. She gasped; she'd found a set of keys hanging from a hook on the cupboard's side.

One of the keys unlocked the gate in the iron fence, and into the cage they went. The torchlight spotlighted the figure on the bed, who made no movement whatsoever. They were wearing a woollen hat, the rest of them hidden beneath the blankets. Even when Etta shook the body gently and pulled back the blanket, shining the light in the figure's face, they did not stir. But what of our two heroines? They stirred, alright; not only that, they gasped and jumped back in horror.

24

WHO'S WHO?

Pale, emaciated, devoid of the positive energy for which she was renowned, Marketa was deep in an unnatural sleep.

"She's been drugged," said Dora.

It took a great deal of calling and shaking and Leon licking her face before the woman slowly stirred, and an age more until she opened her eyes.

"Marketa, dear, wake up, we have to go," said Etta.

"Please try to move a bit," urged Dora.

"Someone has sedated you, and we must get out of here before it's too late and they return." Etta was hoping to elicit some survival instinct in the nurse, but the woman, now sitting up on the camp bed, looked dazed. She just stared at them without recognition.

Etta looked at her phone, disappointed but not surprised to see there was no signal in the depths of the shelter.

"Shall we leave her here and go for help?" she asked.

"What if the killer comes back before help arrives, realises someone has broken in and discovered his nasty little secret, and makes her disappear for good?"

"You're right. We need to get her out of here, even if it will be like dragging a huge bag of potatoes."

Draping Marketa's arms across their shoulders, the two friends stood her up between them and moved forward. The nurse's first steps were stumbling as if her knees couldn't support her at all, then under the continuous blunt urgings of Etta and sweet encouragements from Dora, the woman seemed to regain a little of her senses.

"As soon as we're out into the garden, I'll call for help from everyone," stuttered Etta, sweat pouring down her face, "the police, Christine, Marketa's cousin, our home swap host back in Castelmezzano, Maddalena. The more people who know what has happened, the more confident we can be that corruption won't work against us."

"Oh, I'll be so happy to be out of here," puffed Dora.

They had left the prisoner's cage and were making their way down the long corridor, passing closed doors. Dora prayed they had not dismissed the hypothesis that someone else might be in the shelter too quickly. After all Leon's woofs and their conversations, anyone down here with them would be well aware of their presence.

Dora closed her eyes momentarily, dismissing the thought as she and Etta kept going. But when Etta's torchlight shone on the concrete steps climbing up and out of the bunker, doubt kicked in. How would they drag Marketa all the way up there? The steps were not wide enough to allow the three of them to proceed side by side, as they were doing now.

"One thing at a time," Etta answered as if reading her friend's mind. "Let's get to the steps first."

They were all in a lather by the time they reached the staircase, but to Etta and Dora's relief, they could feel the fresh air coming down from the open hatch. Leon for once was following them, keeping a rear guard and urging them to move quickly. He didn't like the underground space either.

"How shall we drag her up the stairs?" Dora asked as they sat Marketa down on the second step so they could breathe a little.

"Come on, girl," Etta said into the nurse's face. "You've done a splendid job so far. A little more effort and you will be free again, and this nightmare will be over. But you need to react, you have to help us."

For the first time, something like a twinkle gleamed in the nurse's eyes, but it was too dark for the two friends to recognise it.

"Help me stand her up," said Etta. "I'll drape her arms across my shoulders and drag her."

"But you can't!" cried Dora.

"And you will push her bum, and hopefully she will help, too, because if she's a total deadweight, we won't get far. I'm not as strong as I was in my fifties."

Etta knew it would have been pointless to mention the strength she had in her twenties, that was too long ago. But she hoped she might be able to summon the strength of just ten years earlier. Maddalena called it positive thinking; Etta regarded it as brainwashing and had always despised the idea, but necessity is an excellent facilitator of changing one's own mind.

The first six steps were simply awful. Etta feared she might have a stroke right there, then she realised she had just forgotten to breathe. Again, Maddalena and her silly yoga stuff came to mind, the breathing exercises she had tried to teach her mother. It seemed the lessons hadn't been in vain after all.

"I need to pause a little," she cried to Dora behind her. "Just a brief stop." As she straightened her back, still holding Marketa's hands, she felt the woman standing on her own two feet. Or maybe it was just Dora holding her.

Etta breathed deeply. Hoping her time for a stroke had not arrived yet, she thought of the long walks she had done with Dora and Leon to keep fit. She would do this. Life could be a struggle, but struggles had always motivated her.

"OK, let's move on," she cried. "Are you up for it?"

"I am," said Dora, encouraged by her friend's determination. Etta was back to her usual self. As for Leon, he decided it was time he led the line, so he squeezed past the bipeds' legs. From a few steps above, he would turn back every now and then to make sure the three had not rolled catastrophically back down to the sinister underground bunker.

The welcoming fresh air was hitting Etta's face, which was deep red with the effort. The last six steps, and Etta concentrated on each one like a weight lifter raising the barbell above her head, each movement in a perfect sequence, trying to minimise the effort of every single muscle fibre. To use the power of the mind in her favour rather than against her, Etta thought beyond the effort to the reward of freedom. It was funny how in such a difficult moment, Maddalena, her patronising daughter, should be on her radar. The stuff she preached had stuck, hidden somewhere in the back of Etta's brain, and now it came unexpectedly to the rescue.

"What's that?" asked Dora, her voice alarmed. And it was only then that Etta, her face purple with the effort she had been transcending, realised she had been hearing something significant for a while, too: a deep, elongated growl.

When Etta's head finally emerged above ground, the fog had cleared and a veiled moonbeam was hitting Leon's back. His fur was standing up, the growl deepening. When the cloud was moved on by a gust of wind, Etta saw that in front of Leon was a pair of legs. Her eyes slowly made their way up, from the dark boots to the knees, from the waist hidden by a winter jacket to the chest. The face was in shadow, but the moonlight was hitting something in the figure's hand.

A gun.

Worse still, a gun pointing alternately at the Basset, and then at her, across her shoulders to Marketa, and on to Dora coming up close behind them.

"Ahhh, there you are." The hissing voice could have belonged to a man or a woman. "To start with, shut the mutt up or he will be the first to go." Leon's fur bristled even more, but whether it was as a result of the threat or being called a mutt,

Etta didn't know. "I'll be only too happy to get rid of some of you. I don't like large groups."

Etta, now almost three quarters of the way out of the bunker, didn't know how she managed to keep Marketa's hands in hers and not drop them in surprise and horror. But hold on to the nurse she did, at the same time telling Leon to be quiet and come by.

Leon wasn't used to obeying, especially when the order didn't make sense to him.

"Please, Leon," implored Dora, also emerging from the ground. Luckily, she hadn't let go of Marketa when she heard the threat, either, or they would have all tumbled back down the stairs. "Come here."

Leon retreated a little, a hunch telling him that the metal toy the figure was holding had some terrible powers.

"Good girls." The figure sniggered. "Now turn round and back in you go."

"In there?" cried Etta, stunned.

"Exactly."

"I can't do it right now, I need a little rest," and before the figure could say anything, her knees gave way. It was only thanks to Dora that she managed to sit Marketa on the side of the trapdoor with her legs resting on the top steps. The lower half of Dora was still inside the shelter, the upper half helping the nurse to keep her back straight.

"I'll give you exactly 10 seconds before I start to pick you off." The gun was aimed at Leon.

"Thirty seconds!" cried Etta. "And then we'll go back down without a fuss."

"Nine," said the figure with little pause between one number and the next, "eight... seven..."

"Go down, Leon, catch it!" And Etta threw her bag into the bunker, hoping that the dog would for once be tempted to retrieve it, a game he generally despised. After a second's hesitation, Leon went down to fetch the object.

"Six... five..."

Quickly, Etta grabbed Marketa. Luckily, the woman's knees were strong enough to support her. But the nurse hesitated as if she didn't want to go down into the darkness, not again.

"Four..."

"You should make allowances for our age, you moron," cried Etta, pushing Marketa into Dora's arms, and then trying to follow them below ground, but finding the way blocked by the slowness of the other two.

"Three... two... o..."

Etta tensed, ready for the bullet to hit her back. How would it feel? Would she have time to think or would her life fly away before she'd even realised she was dead? What if it inflicted a mortal wound, but not immediate death? Would she be lying on the ground, suffering, breathing her last in the arms of Dora and the paws of Leon? Would their grief for her be too much for them to bear?

Then she heard the gun discharge and closed her eyes before the bullet reached her. She expected to feel a terrible pain, waiting for it to come, but there was nothing. Maybe she had died on the spot. Then she realised two things: one, she was still standing on her feet, and two, instead of a BOOM, what she had heard was more like a THUMP!

Etta opened her eyes. Her feet were on the sixth step down, only her head was emerging from the trap door. And there, at ground level, she found herself face to face with Marketa's nasty neighbour. She let out a cry, only to realise he was lying on the ground, his eyes shut, his face contorted into a grimace, clearly unconscious.

Etta's eyes travelled upwards, falling on the figure of Mr Janda with a hoe in his hands. He looked at her as if he couldn't believe what he'd done. Was he going to hit her, too?

"How is she? How is Marketa?" he asked, letting the hoe slide from his hands. Etta realised he was closer to fainting than striking out.

"I don't know," she exhaled a sigh of relief. "But she's alive, and you just saved our lives, too... Dora, wait! Let me help you out."

"Is that beast no longer threatening to shoot us?"

"He's been knocked out, Mr Janda has come to the rescue."

"Yes," the man said. "Let me help you."

"No, you stay there. We'll push Marketa forward and you can pull her out."

As Mr Janda knelt down to help, Etta and Dora struggled on the steps to turn and push Marketa back up. Although the nurse was now standing on her own two feet, she was still as rigid as an automaton and as vacuous as a zombie.

"I hope she will come back to reality sometime," Etta murmured, uncharacteristic sympathy for the nurse enveloping her. But her charitable thoughts didn't last long. Someone else was approaching from up above, and they didn't sound happy. At all.

The newcomer spoke, a sinister tone to their voice. "Well done. What a great team of sleuths!"

25

YOU CAN TEACH A YOUNG POLICEMAN OLD TRICKS

"Yes, it's me, come to... *help out*," said the new arrival. Etta glanced at Mr Janda, who was standing stock still, silent, rigid.

How should I play this? she thought, deciding to feign ignorance.

"Great, so now there are two men to help Marketa. We'll just sit her here on the steps and you two can come and take over. I'm exhausted."

"I don't think so," said the newcomer, "but I can certainly send Mr Janda down to comfort you."

The voice did not sound as cheeky as usual. Etta turned to see what was happening. And there was Mike Smolak threatening Josef Janda, a gun in his hands.

"Please go back down, 'Mrs Fletcher'. I've come to help out my colleague," and he nodded his head towards the prone body of Marketa's nasty neighbour. "I thought you'd have worked it out by now; maybe I overestimated you and you're just a couple of gossipy old harridans after all."

"Mr Smolak?" Dora had sat Marketa on the steps and come up to see for herself what was happening. "Not you! But why?"

"There's no time for explanations," Smolak said, pushing

Janda towards the trapdoor. "Now, down you go or I'll have to start the shooting earlier than I planned."

The two women would have hurried down into the bunker were it not for the fact that Mr Janda had joined them on the top step. Their bodies, being on the plump side while the hatch was far too narrow, had got stuck by the time they'd turned around. With their legs safely below ground, their upper bodies were dangerously exposed to the threat of bullets.

Who will he start with? Etta thought as Smolak lowered his gun. Leon started to bark from further down the steps, Marketa's body cutting off his access to the exit. The brave dog would have come to the rescue otherwise, not that he could have done much. But couldn't the wretched man get on with his shooting and have it done with? This was the second time a gun had been trained on her today and the sun had barely risen; it was enough to kill her without the use of a bullet. Once you know you're going to die, surely it's the sooner, the better, isn't it? Or where there is life, is there really hope?

But why wasn't he shooting?

Etta slowly opened her right eye. The man wasn't there. She then opened her left eye.

Smolak was kneeling down meekly, facing Etta. Without looking at her, he laid his gun on the ground. Only then did Etta see another man had arrived, previously hidden by Smolak. He was holding something that looked pretty much like a branch against Smolak's back, and the older man clearly believed it to be a weapon of some kind.

Etta recognised him instantly: the young man who'd been following them the night they'd had dinner with Marketa. Their attacker. What the heck was happening?

Smolak pushed the weapon behind him. As the younger man kneeled to pick it up, Smolak must have felt the pressure of the 'weapon' diminish slightly and, as the attention of his adversary was distracted, he took his chance. Turning suddenly, he kicked the man below the chest, leaving him breathless for a few seconds.

Smolak tried to snatch the gun from the young man's hands, but the other managed to launch it away from them as the two rolled in the grass, one then the other gaining the upper position, fighting hard. In the meantime, Dora, Etta and Janda had finally freed themselves from the hatch and were helping each other out.

"What should we do?" cried Mr Janda, seeing the two men fighting.

"Just make sure he doesn't wake up," said Etta, handing Mr Janda a geranium pot and nodding towards the mean old man who was coming to his senses, his first view as his eyes opened being a heavy terracotta vase suspended above his head.

"Where's the other gun?" said Etta, searching all around the old man. Smolak and the young man were still fighting, striking blows as if they were stuntmen in a cheap action movie where there's no end to the number of hits and misses.

"That gun?" Mr Janda asked, tapping Etta repeatedly on her shoulder. Annoyed by the man's insistence, Etta raised her eyes and saw Lieutenant Baloun grinning at her, the old man's gun in his hand. Looking at the two fighting men as if he were refereeing a wrestling match, he seemed determined not to intervene, no matter what.

"Lieutenant Baloun, what's happening?" Etta cried, the word 'betrayal' hacking at the inside of her head like a jackhammer. But the policeman's response surprised her.

"I want to see if this lad has learned anything of use in these modern academies."

At that moment, the young chap finally managed to block Smolak. A knee on his back, he recited the words advising him of his rights, placing handcuffs on his wrists before standing him up in one smooth manoeuvre. Baloun, in the meantime, had done the same with Marketa's neighbour.

When the young man came forward, Etta could contain herself no more.

"Be careful! This is the man who attacked us the day we visited Marketa."

"Come on, Mrs Fletcher," Baloun reproached her. "You can do better than that."

Etta's eyes went to Smolak. "Well, I had come to the conclusion that he was Ms Eva Kladivova's murderer, but I thought the mysterious attacker might have been his partner in crime, primed to deflect suspicion from Smolak when he apparently came to our rescue..."

"The truth, I'm afraid, is much worse than that," said the Lieutenant, glancing with a saddened face at the young policeman, who flushed.

"I see," said Etta triumphantly. "You had him follow us to protect us. But that means you never believed Ms Kladivova's death was due to a robbery that ended badly."

"No," the Lieutenant admitted. "I never believed that, but I didn't want to encourage your theorising, either, as I was afraid you'd go about, stirring murky waters and landing yourself in trouble. When Pavel Kraus – this young policeman here – was caught by Mr Smolak, I really thought the man had tried to protect you, too. But then I got a little suspicious... as young and inexperienced as Kraus is, his antagonist seemed to know a few tricks that you learn either in the police force..."

"...or in the STB," Etta finished for him.

"That's correct," Baloun winked at her. "But how about we take care of poor Marketa Ciprova, lock these scoundrels up, and meet later to tie up the loose ends, exactly as happens in the movies?"

"For once, I'm going to do exactly what you advise, Lieutenant."

~

"MRS FLETCHER!" LIEUTENANT BALOUN REGARDED HER WITH A WRY smile. "You're most definitely a force of nature. How did you come to these conclusions?"

"The picture in Marketa's flat," Etta answered, pushing her large red-framed glasses back up her nose.

"The missing picture?" Christine asked. They were all sitting in a private hospital room around Marketa's bed. The retired nurse was still weak, but was much better than she had been, according to doctors.

"That's it," Etta answered. "The killer didn't want us to notice something significant about that picture and I started to wonder why."

"But you said," Christine insisted, "that Mr Smolak didn't even appear in the picture..."

"Exactly."

"I don't understand. If he wasn't in the picture, what did he have to fear about it? Why take it?"

All eyes converged on Etta, who was undoubtedly enjoying being the centre of attention.

"There are two reasons why the killer wouldn't want people to take notice of that picture," she said, ramping up the suspense. "Either because he was in it, or because he wasn't."

As she'd expected, a sea of blank faces looked back at her. All except Baloun. He... he knew.

"At the Embassy," she continued after a long, studied pause, "the official picture framed and shown in the library includes Mr Smolak, but strangely, neither Mrs Temple Black nor Marketa had chosen that one for their own personal mementoes. Was it just coincidence, or did both women have their reasons to exclude him? And of those two women, the one who was still alive had disappeared in an ocean of lies that was completely out of character..."

Marketa sat in her bed, propped up against a pile of pillows, still pale, although a streak of pink was making its way back on to her cheeks as the hours passed by. She was listening to the story as if it concerned someone else. Only occasionally did her eyes leave Etta to wander to the pretty bouquet on her bedside table.

"You are a genius, madam," said Baloun. "You were on the tracks of a man because he was *not* portrayed in a picture. Whatever next?"

"The cables, we asked the Embassy if we could read the cables that Mrs Shirley Temple Black sent to Washington. We actually could not, but Christine inadvertently left a folder on her desk... and I'm afraid we snooped a little."

"Of course," said the Lieutenant, grinning. Christine opened her mouth as if shocked at the revelation, as if she'd never imagined these two dear women could be capable of such duplicity. Shaking her head, she then winked at Dora, whose cheeks were on fire.

"Someone," Etta carried on, "was relaying private conversations held inside the US Embassy back to the secret police. Women are instinctive creatures – what if both Marketa and Mrs Temple Black had rejected the photograph which included Mr Smolak as they did not trust him? Despite his apparent support for the dissidents, despite him playing an important role in the Velvet Revolution, he was moved by the Embassy into a position where he would have less access to delicate information. The man had served the Embassy faithfully – officially, that could not be denied him – but twenty-six years later, we find him in the Department of Commerce, not among the trusted Embassy staff."

Marketa nodded. "That's all true. We never voiced our suspicions, but by tacit agreement, we avoided discussing sensitive topics when he was around. But why would he want to kill Eva Kladivova?"

"That's related to a sad story," sighed Etta, "that Brother Benedikt told us. And I'm sure, Marketa, you too are familiar with parts of it. We need to go back to the mid-1980s. Mr Smolak wasn't working for the Embassy at the time, but in

Prague, the dissidents' voices were starting to be heard. More and more people had signed Charter 77, the winds of change had begun their dance, shyly at first before becoming stronger and stronger.

"Then in 1985, Eva Kladivova's brother was killed by the STB during a brutal interrogation. She was there and witnessed it all. I believe Mr Smolak was in charge of the operation, and conducted the interrogation, too. I have no doubt the torturers hid their identities just in case – you know, wearing balaclavas over their faces. But after the concert, during the event at the theatre, I believe something struck Eva, reminded her of that terrible time. Maybe it was Smolak's voice, maybe those roguish blue eyes. It was the first time they had met in person, and there and then, she knew she was facing the man who'd killed her brother."

"That's when you caught her looking at Mr Janda?" Baloun asked.

"I thought she was looking at Mr Janda, but I guess she was just looking round the room, maybe trying to tear her attention away from her brother's murderer. The look on her face was a result of the awful epiphany she'd had; Mr Janda just happened to be in its path."

"That's all correct," Baloun confirmed, bowing to Etta. "Mr Smolak has confessed to it all: Eva Kladivova *had* recognised him. When she went drinking with the three men after they had left the theatre, she told him she needed to speak to him, alone. It was then that he realised he might have been too bold. Had she realised who he was, even after all those years?"

"You mean he knew all along who she was?"

"Of course. But as he had been acting incognito during the eighties, he was confident no one would recognise him, apart from his former colleagues like Miss Ciprova's neighbour."

"Then what happened?" Christine asked.

"When they left the bar, they parted at the Legii Bridge, but Smolak doubled back and joined Eva, as she had asked. She told him she had recognised him as her brother's killer, that she was going to denounce him…"

"Would that have mattered?" Dora asked. Plenty of former STB operatives had been reintegrated into Czech society.

"Indeed, it would have been a scandal. He might not have been working for the Embassy any more, but to have a brutal STB killer in a key role in the US Department of Commerce… I believe it would have ruined him. Our American cousins are pretty strict when it comes to ethical behaviour – he risked being sacked just before he reached retirement age and drew on a good pension. And his family, who had for the most part been ignorant of his real role in the past, would have had to face the shame."

"But why did she tell him? Why alert him?"

"She made the big mistake of being too self-confident. Feeling sure the man wouldn't have time to act, and because they were in the city centre, she didn't realise that by simply asking him to meet with her, she had given away the fact that she had rumbled him. And Smolak had been trained to act fast under adverse circumstances. It was in his DNA as an STB agent – always have a weapon with you, keep your emotions in check and do what has to be done.

"In seconds, he was back into his old role as a ruthless secret police officer. He listened and pretended to be shocked by her accusations, but as she turned to walk to her hotel, he leapt on her, stabbing her in the back and throwing her from the bridge before she realised what was happening."

Dora looked down at the hound by her feet. "It's odd that Leon liked Mr Smolak, a lot," she said pensively.

"The man is a skilful liar," Etta replied. "But it has to be said that Leon wasn't fooled – he was the one to take us straight to him."

"What?" Dora and Lieutenant Baloun asked her simultaneously.

"The morning that poor Ms Kladivova's body was found,

after we'd identified her, at the southern end of the Kampa park, Leon started to pull towards the bridge. He had recognised the same smell he'd found near the body, so he took us to where the killer had returned to the scene of his crime. I guess Smolak wanted to make sure the body hadn't been found, so he walked all the way down the bridge on the left bank, then he came back to return to his room at the Smetana Hotel. And Leon, once he found the trail on the left bank, followed it across the bridge. After our breakfast at Café Slavia, we passed in front of the Smetana Hotel, and there he caught the fresh trail Smolak had left that very morning. Thus he found his man..."

"...back at the crime scene!" Dora cried.

"Apparently, it's true. Killers always return..."

"That's why," Dora thought aloud, cutting Baloun off, "Leon greeted Mr Smolak so enthusiastically: he wasn't pleased because he liked him; he'd actually reached his prey."

Well, Leon admitted to himself, *I might have misjudged the man a little, but my nose didn't betray me. I found the killer before anyone else.*

"Such an impudent man," Dora said. "He always seemed to be so friendly, even acknowledging he could be considered one of the suspects..."

"I believe," Etta said, "he realised other people would make more obvious suspects. He knew Mr Janda's company was suffering because of the competition from Ms Kladivova's; he knew she and her former husband still argued, and in the eyes of the police, people close to the victim are often the first suspects. I'm not sure he knew about the will, but once he found out, he must have felt more reassured than ever."

"Unfortunately," Baloun said, "he also knew you were looking into the past. He was aware that Marketa had never trusted him, and when he saw the two of you befriending her..."

Leon barked in protest.

"You're right," acknowledged the Lieutenant. "The *three* of you befriending Marketa, he feared she would reveal her suspicions about him. And that made him realise he had to act fast. Since one of his former men lived opposite Marketa, they got together and drew up a plan to kidnap the nurse and hide her in the old nuclear bunker in the garden."

"But why not just kill her?" Etta said, glancing apologetically at Marketa. "Wouldn't that have been safer and simpler?"

"I believe I was saved by pure chance," Marketa said. "When we were all serving at the Embassy, Smolak's baby daughter got sick. I recognised the symptoms of leukaemia and told him to take her to the hospital immediately. It was a tough time for him, but I also referred the baby to some experienced colleagues of mine and they managed to save her. Maybe he felt he couldn't kill me after that."

"Without a doubt, that's what saved your life," Baloun said, caressing his moustache.

"But how could he ever set Marketa free," Christine asked, "when she could tell the police she'd been held prisoner near her own home?"

"I had no idea where I was," said Marketa. "I had been drugged so heavily, I felt like I was being driven for hours before we arrived at my prison."

"And you never saw who was holding you prisoner," Etta added.

"I never thought I was right opposite my own home, nor that my neighbour was my jailor."

"Smolak was planning to have you released a few days after he had safely returned to the US," confirmed Baloun.

"I confess," said Marketa, "that in the pleasure of seeing everyone again after so many years, I never thought of Mr Smolak as a potential killer. When Etta and Dora came to speak to me, I didn't suspect for a moment that Eva Kladivova's death had anything to do with the past. It's true I never liked Smolak, but without proof that he was the one leaking information to the STB, I sometimes thought maybe I was being unfair to him."

"The thing that still puzzles me," said Etta, "is that all those people converged on the nuclear bunker just in the nick of time. What was Mr Janda doing there? And Pavel Kraus, and you yourself, Lieutenant?"

As if on cue, there was a light knock on the door and Mr Janda's head popped around it.

"Josef, please come in," Marketa invited him, her cheeks gaining a little more colour. The man blushed at seeing so many people there, but he greeted them all.

"More flowers, Josef?" said Marketa, nodding towards the orchid he was carrying, along with a box of chocolates and a little present.

"This time I chose a plant so you can take it back home with you…"

"How lovely," she said, looking at the glossy dark green leaves and the large, mesmerising flowers.

"And a little book," he said, handing her the wrapped gift, "so that you've got something to read while you're in hospital."

"That's so nice of you."

"Well, Mr Janda, you're just in time," said Baloun. "We were wondering what you were doing in Nový Svět early this morning?"

If the man had blushed earlier on, now his face was crimson.

"I made a mistake," he said, looking Etta and Dora up and down. "I had seen you both around Marketa's home on a number of occasions and I wondered what you were up to. You had been with her the night Eva died, and you'd been the last ones to see Marketa before she vanished. I thought you'd made up the story of being attacked to divert attention from your activities."

"You mean you thought we were involved?"

"Exactly. When I followed you to Karlštejn, I thought you wanted to convince Marketa's cousin that she had gone away of her own free will…"

"But we actually went to prove the exact opposite!" protested Etta.

"I know... that is, now I know. But at the time... Also, when I told Lieutenant Baloun that maybe you were up to something underhand... well... he didn't really dismiss my ideas..."

All eyes rolled on to Baloun.

"Well, you should thank me for that. That way, I would be free to investigate the murder without interference as you would be too busy checking on one another."

"I don't want to know what you told Mr Zima!"

"Not much," Baloun waved his hands dismissively. "He was only interested in visiting his daughter from his first marriage and his grandchildren; he had no interest in sleuthing."

"So you knew Mr Janda was keeping an eye on us while we tried to solve the crime. And what about your policeman, Pavel Kraus? Did you call him off and leave it to Mr Janda, or was he still following us, too?"

"No, I told him that from then on, it'd be Mr Janda following you and he could take a break. But the lad is young and has the energy to go drinking late into the night after work. He was leaving a bar in Nový Svět when he saw Mr Janda climbing over a wall into a garden opposite Miss Ciprova's house, and then disappearing on the other side."

"That's why Kraus had no gun with him – he was off duty?"

"That's right, it was just a happy accident."

"How about you, Lieutenant? How did you happen to be there?"

"The young lad had been making so many mistakes that this time, he decided for once to do the right thing. Before climbing over the wall, he had the good sense to give me a call. We had just uncovered Smolak's sinister past, and we knew he was in touch with his former colleague, Marketa's neighbour; we just needed some evidence to be able to apply for a search warrant."

"Really?" Etta was shocked; she had never thought the police could be so smart. In fact, at one point, she had even suspected that Baloun could be the murderer – a man who had been seen around the Embassy back in the eighties, but no one had noticed him because he was a local policeman. But she need not confess to any of this; she didn't want to spoil her perfect reputation as the new Mrs Fletch... Jane Rizzoli.

"Last ten minutes for visitors," a nurse called from the door. She was about to go about her business when she did a double take. "Um, is that a dog?"

"Doesn't look much like a lion, does he?" said Baloun, widening his eyes in shocked innocence as if he too had just spotted Leon for the first time.

The nurse gave him a dirty look. "Dogs are not allowed in hospitals."

"I know," Baloun said sweetly, "but he's a service dog. When we arrived, I showed his credentials at the reception." And he waved a police badge and a sheaf of papers that had nothing to do with dogs at all, let alone service dogs.

The woman looked at him incredulously. "Ten minutes left," she said and then withdrew, barely concealing her smile.

Dora jumped up immediately and, with an uncharacteristic dose of determination and assertiveness, said her farewells to Marketa and ushered everyone out of the room. Well, almost everyone. As Etta protested, Dora got her revenge for the day of their visit to the Embassy and kicked her hard in the shin.

"We need to give them some time alone," she explained once she had hustled her friend outside.

"Who?" Etta replied. Turning round, she realised Mr Janda wasn't with them. "You don't mean the poor woman is going to be manipulated into a relationship in a moment of weakness?"

"They will make a beautiful couple," Dora replied gently, patting her disgruntled friend on the back just as she'd normally pat Leon.

EPILOGUE

A nd the terrible day came when the trio had to leave Prague.

The evening before their departure, Leon waited for Guendaline to appear at the window opposite so they could wish each other goodnight for the last time. She looked prettier than ever – could he really leave her? The poor hound spent the whole night pondering on the right thing to do. On one side were those two rotund women he had adopted in Rothenburg; on the other was the sweetest, daintiest, most charming she-Basset who'd ever walked the earth.

Maybe it was time for Leon to think of his own life, start a family. After all, he had taught his two ladies a lot. And in truth, both had made quite a bit of progress: the Etta-biped was still a bit on the stubborn side, but she was so much nicer than she used to be. Of course, the sour part of her was a matter of genetics and DNA, so he couldn't expect too much. As for the Dora-biped, she was definitely more self-confident than before.

He sighed. He had to admit he'd miss them, but still, they could come to Prague and visit Guendaline and him whenever they pleased. They'd always find room in his new flat. He'd announce his decision to them in the morning, when Guendaline and her biped came by for the big farewell.

His resolution made, Leon fell asleep, dreaming of walks in Petřín park and back to the flat, walks on Kampa island and back to the flat, all the time with Guendaline at his side...

~

WHEN LEON WOKE UP THE NEXT MORNING, DORA WAS PREPARING toast for breakfast while the two women chattered endlessly as usual.

"I have the perfect itinerary," Dora was announcing. "A home swapper will be happy for us to stay at their place in Koblenz for three nights. I wonder if the town will be as nice as Rothenburg."

No way! Leon dismissed the very idea. No German town could be as quaint as his native Rothenburg ob der Tauber, but certainly, there were other OK places. Like Prague...

"Then we're off to Calais," Dora continued, showing the route to Etta, who seemed unusually peaceful and happy. "I've found a reasonably priced B&B. Early the next morning, we'll take the Eurotunnel and..."

"Just imagine it, Dora, traversing the Channel, staying in Calais," and Etta clasped her hands and opened her mouth, mimicking her friend.

"Don't tease me!" Dora protested softly, slapping Etta's hands.

"In fact," admitted Etta, squeezing her friend's arm, "I confess I'm thrilled, too. Who would imagine we'd drive all that way?"

The two jigged happily. Leon frowned. He wasn't familiar with Channels and Eurotunnels, but they sounded vaguely interesting.

"I hope our first stop in the UK won't require much driving," said Etta. "I still cannot understand why the British, who one would think of as decent people, should insist on driving on the wrong side of the road..."

If Leon hadn't made up his mind to stay in Prague, he would have loved to visit the UK. Lots of people had told him he was as smart as an English lord, so he was sure there had to be some aristocratic blood running through his veins...

"We'll be stopping in Cambridge, just a couple of hours from the Eurotunnel, maybe three. Then finally, we're travelling up to Scotland."

Scotland? That was a name that had always sent shivers of anticipation through the hound's body, some kind of ancestral call... but no! He mustn't allow himself to be distracted. He'd made his mind up – he'd stay in Prague, walk through Petřín and Kampa park every single day accompanied by the cutest she-Bassett...

"Such a splendid idea our hosts have had," Dora continued, opening a little booklet containing a few photographs of remote stone cottages, endless moors and a map, "to suggest we leave our car and luggage at their parents' house in Glasgow and walk the West Highland Way. A ten-day hike in the Scottish wilderness before we reach Fort William and the highest peaks in the UK."

Ten days' hiking? Those two, who had trouble finding the door to a building in the centre of Prague? The mere thought sent shivers through the Basset's body.

The doorbell rang.

"My goodness, that must be Guendaline and her owner," said Dora, rushing to answer the intercom and inviting the two upstairs.

～

SUCH IS LIFE. LEON WAS DEEP IN MELANCHOLY THOUGHTS AS HE SAT in the back of Dora's Fiat 500, watching the last pretty buildings of Prague fade out of sight in the distance. *A poor fellow only gets to choose which path of regret he wants to walk. In this cruel world, there's no route to complete happiness.* He would never forget the look on Guendaline's face as they'd parted. Oh, his love, his one true love!

At that moment, the view opened up on to the green stripes of fields and the trees in blossom, the sky a perfect blue with just a few fluffy clouds. Dora opened her window a couple of inches, the breeze enough to send Leon's ears flapping, his nostrils quivering at the strange intoxicating smell making its way into the car.

His heart all of a sudden felt light as euphoria invaded him. He had recognised the scent of new adventures to come!

∾

I REALLY HOPE YOU ENJOYED THIS BOOK. IS THERE ANY WAY A **reader may help an author? Yes! Please leave a review on Amazon, Goodreads and/or Bookbub.** It doesn't matter how long or short; even a single sentence could say it all. We might be in a digital era, but **this old world of ours still revolves around word of mouth**. A review allows a book to leave the shadow of the unknown and introduces it to other passionate readers.

GRAZIE :)

MORE BOOKS FROM ADRIANA LICIO

THE HOMESWAPPERS SERIES

0 - Castelmezzano, The Witch Is Dead – Prequel to the series

1 - The Watchman of Rothenburg Dies: A German Travel Mystery

2 - A Wedding and A Funeral in Mecklenburg : A German Cozy Mystery

3 - An Aero Island Christmas Mystery: A Danish Cozy Mystery

4 – Prague, A Secret From The Past: A Czech Travel Mystery

5 – Death on the West Highland Way: A Scottish Travel Mystery - coming in 2022

AN ITALIAN VILLAGE MYSTERY SERIES

0 - And Then There Were Bones. The prequel to the *An Italian Village Mystery* series is **available for free by signing up to www.adrianalicio.com/murderclub**

1 - Murder on the Road Returning to her quaint hometown in Italy following the collapse of her engagement, feisty travel writer Giò Brando just wants some peace and quiet. Instead, she finds herself a suspect in a brutal murder.

2 A Fair Time for Death is a mystery set during the Autumn

Chestnut Fair in Trecchina, a mountain village near Maratea, involving a perfume with a split personality, a disappearing corpse, a disturbing secret from the past and a mischievous goat.

3 - A Mystery Before Christmas A haunting Christmas song from a faraway land. A child with striking green eyes. A man with no past. A heartwarming mystery for those who want to breathe in the delicious scents and flavours of a Mediterranean December.

4 - Peril at the Pellicano Hotel – A group of wordsmiths, a remote hotel. Outside, the winds howl and the seas rage. But the real danger lurks within.

More books to come in Autumn 2021

AUTHOR'S NOTE

In spring 2018, my hubby, Frodo the dog and I enjoyed a wonderful home swap in Prague. Our flat in Malostranské náměstí contained a grand piano, underneath which became the favourite spot for Frodo's naps. When he was awake, we'd often find him, forelegs on the windowsill, staring across at another dog in the flat opposite. How they were communicating and what they were saying to each other remains a mystery to this day.

We visited lots of tourist places. As sophisticated as we pretend to be – not very, really – we couldn't skip those as they're simply charming. Tourists are no fools! But we stayed in Prague long enough to be able to explore some lesser known areas. Mind you, we shamelessly took any opportunity to walk across the Charles Bridge, every hour of every day.

Frodo quickly became an expert in the art of spotting green parks wherever we went. Of all the many in Prague, Kampa Island, with its amazing views over the Vltava and explosion of lilacs, became one of our favourite places, not least because of its open-air café serving good food and excellent cakes.

Early one morning, I noticed a striking-looking woman clothed in a dramatic red dress. The image haunted my memory for months afterwards until I could make good use of her – on second thoughts, maybe 'good use' isn't quite the right term for a murder victim. Alas, I'm just a poor mystery writer!

On another occasion, a couple of friends invited us to a concert of traditional Korean music, where we were introduced to the South Korean Ambassador and his wife.

I'm telling you all this to acknowledge that the poor opinion Etta has of writers as lazy good-for-nothings might be partly justified. Stories are, for the most part, all around us, so we authors don't have to do that much in terms of creation. We just recount real life and add a few spices...

Amongst the spices I've used are, of course, a selection of books I've had the pleasure of reading, detailed later in these notes. As for the main ingredient – well, for that, I admit I had to work a little harder. I needed a central theme that would bring the places we had visited to life and, more ambitiously, set the story against a backdrop of Prague's past. Because you can't visit Prague and ignore its history; there's so much to learn about humanity, hope and darkness.

At the same time, I know my limits. I'm a cheerful soul, easily put off by the more brutal side of life. How could I marry the grim past of Communism and oppression with the positivity of a cosy? I searched and searched, I read and read, but for the life of me, I couldn't find what I was looking for. Out of despair, I put down the books, ceased the internet searches and looked for a podcast on Prague.

Rick Steves is a treasure trove to me. He's insightful, the best incarnation of the curious tourist. But this time, even he didn't seem to have what I needed. Then on the podcast of a Prague radio station, I literally stumbled upon an interview with a former US Ambassador in the city who'd written a book about the Embassy and its most famous Ambassador, Mrs Shirley Temple Black. Shirley Temple? The blonde curly-top whose movies I adored when I was a kid? She was an Ambassador, in Prague, in 1989? Really? I had to know more, and more than that, I needed to use my findings to craft a decent story.

To my deepest regret, I didn't get the opportunity to mention Josefov, Prague's Jewish quarter, in this book. I've tried many times to include it, but it seems out of place in my story, even though visiting it was one of the most moving moments during our walks around the city. I will never forget the power of the walls in the Pinkas Synagogue, covered in the names of the 80,000 Czech Jews who died during the Holocaust, nor the quiet intimacy of the Josefov graveyard where hundreds of tombstones are crammed into a little green space, or the dystopian sense of the Jewish Town Hall with its clock running anticlockwise. Maybe Josefov will be the setting for a second mystery in Prague. Maybe it will be the reason why Etta, Dora and Leon return... besides Guendaline, of course!

Books to read about Prague

Norman Eisen, former US Ambassador in Prague from 2011 to 2014, wrote two books about the history of the Embassy. *The Last Palace: Europe's turbulent century in five lives and one legendary house* reads like a page-turner novel. It documents Shirley Temple Black's times at the Embassy, starting with the strange coincidence that meant she was there in 1968 when the Soviets invaded the city and put a dramatic end to the celebrated Prague Spring. The other book – *Democracy's Defenders: US Embassy Prague, the fall of Communism in Czechoslovakia, and its aftermath* – is more factual, showing declassified cables exchanged between the Prague Embassy and Washington in the months before and during the Velvet Revolution. This is fascinating as you get to feel the tone of the cables, reading first-hand the worries, tactics and emotions of the time.

Lonely Planet's *Prague Itineraries* – I cannot find an English edition, but in Spanish, French and Italian, this is an unusual guide to Prague by Guillaume Sorel and Christine Coste. It reads almost like a graphic novel with many anecdotes and beautiful drawings that have a dark, almost Gothic touch. In truth, this mood suits the romantic and mysterious city very well. Highly recommended, even just for an armchair traveller.

Life in Prague

If you're not new to *The Homeswappers Mysteries* series, you might already know that my favourite travel books are written by people who actually move to a new country, experiencing all its idiosyncrasies, good and bad, as compared to the country they've come from.

In researching this novel, I've enjoyed two books by Rachael Weiss who was born in Australia, but went to live in Prague for a year to experience the country from which her family had fled during the communist regime. *Me, Myself and Prague: An unreliable guide to Bohemia* tells the story of this year amongst expats and family members in a country still coping with liberalisation. A year later, Rachael felt the experience had been such a success, she had almost become a misfit in Australia. She moved back to Prague, this time (almost!) for good, as she describes in her second book, *The Thing About Prague: How I gave it all up for a new life in Europe's most eccentric city.*

Of course, both books are memoirs and not travel guides, impregnated with the author's efforts to give meaning and direction to her life. But it's in reading about fits and misfits that I find the real experience of living in Prague, the character of its inhabitants (such as the legendary rudeness of waiters, countered by the strong bonds Weiss forged with distant family members she'd never met before), rather than in a long list of monuments. Weiss's writing style is self-effacing and witty, which makes for entertaining reading – imagine Bridget Jones landing in the middle of the Czech Republic hoping to find Prince Charming while writing the book of a lifetime, and that's besides having to cope with an entirely different system of work, life and bureaucracy.

(Cosy) Mysteries set in Prague

The only Cosy Mystery that I could find set in Prague is *The Doctor Dines in Prague* by Robin Hathaway. Book 4 in the *Dr Fenimore Mysteries* series, it's a fun cosy, taking you around the castle and main monuments of Prague, and it's so delightful that children can enjoy it, too (if they are keen on mysteries *à la Nancy Drew*, that is). As usual, if you find any other cosy mysteries set in Prague, please send me a note.

If you have an eclectic taste in reading material, the good news is that, although there are few cosies set in Prague, there are plenty of mysteries and thrillers (and horror, too). I prefer the ones with less graphic violence, so I enjoyed Graham Brack's *Josef Slonsky Investigation* series enormously. These are witty procedurals featuring a detective with a weird sense of humour, along with plenty of Prague landmarks and food. And as Slonsky worked half of his police life during the Communist regime, there are references to the past, too.

In all honesty, I didn't particularly like the ending of Book 1, *Lying and Dying*, but then I read Book 3, *Death on Duty*, and simply loved it. From there, I went back to Book 1 and found I could put up with the ending in retrospect. In fact, I plan to read the other books in the series. (I'm only saying this in case you're put off reading the other books by the same thing. Or maybe you'll enjoy Book 1, ending included – you're welcome to let me know!)

Contact me on me@adrianalicio.com

ABOUT THE AUTHOR

Adriana Licio lives in the Apennine Mountains in southern Italy, not far from Maratea, the seaside setting for her first cosy series, *An Italian Village Mystery.*

She loves loads of things: travelling, reading, walking, good food, small villages, and homeswapping. A long time ago, she spent six years falling in love with Scotland, and she has never recovered. She now runs her family perfumery, and between a dark patchouli and a musky rose, she devours cosy mysteries.

She resisted writing as long as she could, fearing she might get carried away by her fertile imagination. But one day, she found an alluring blank page and the words flowed in the weird English she'd learned in Glasgow.

Adriana finds peace for her restless, enthusiastic soul by walking in nature with her adventurous golden retriever Frodo and her hubby Giovanni.

Do you want to know more?
Join the **Maratea Murder Club**

You can also stay in touch on:
www.adrianalicio.com

<<<<>>>>

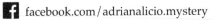

facebook.com/adrianalicio.mystery

twitter.com/adrianalici

amazon.com/author/adrianalicio

bookbub.com/authors/adriana-licio

32490843R00132